Faceless

AMMA DARKO

Faceless

With an introductory essay by
Kofi Anyidoho

SUB-SAHARAN PUBLISHERS

First published in Ghana 2003, by
SUB-SAHARAN PUBLISHERS
P. O. BOX 358
LEGON, ACCRA

Revised edition 2004

ISBN 9988-550-50-2

Design by Anne Y. Sakyi (Sub-Saharan Publishers)

CONTENTS

Amma Darko's *Faceless:*
A New Landmark in Ghanaian Fiction

an introductory essay

by **Kofi Anyidoho**

Students and scholars of African Literature who, like me, have often wondered about the apparent absence of any major female Ghanaian writers following the remarkable pioneering work of Efua T. Sutherland and Ama Ata Aidoo, can now rest assured that a worthy successor has emerged in the person of Amma Darko. With the publication of her third novel, Amma Darko has demonstrated a clear commitment to a productive career in creative writing. Her very first novel was published in a German translation in 1991 under the title *Der Verkaufte Traum*, and was published in its English original in the Heinemann African Writers Series in 1995 as *Beyond the Horizon* and in French as *Parde la L'Horizon*. A decade or so later, we now pay homage to her third novel, simply and ominously titled *Faceless*, again being published in English and in German and Spanish translations. In between *Beyond the Horizon* and *Faceless*, we have *The Housemaid*, also published in both a German translation and in the Heinemann African Writers Series in 1998. There is more than ample evidence that these three works constitute an important trilogy and must be read as such.

The first two novels have already attracted enthusiastic critical attention, most of it focusing on Amma Darko's considerable skill in portraying the plight of women and young girls in a merciless world dominated by greedy, irresponsible and often cruel men in their life. In this brief introductory statement, I wish particularly to draw attention to the fact that taken together, these three novels by Amma Darko tell one long and disturbing tale. Sadly, it is a tale of a diseased society that seems to have lost its hold on the life of its children. It is a provocative tale of a society that has developed a tragic ability of guiding its young ones, especially the girl-child, into a life dedicated to prostituting every conceivable virtue for the sake of flimsy material possessions.

Even as a first novel, *Beyond the Horizon* made immediate and startling impact, as much for the timeliness and urgency of its subject and message, as for the shocking freshness/frankness of the narrative style and voice. Described by one reader as "a natural storyteller's compelling and sobering account of the ruthless exploitation of women in Africa and Europe", *Beyond the Horizon* introduces the theme of society and family's complicity in pushing the vulnerable individual woman /girl into various forms of exploitation and abuse.

Akobi, the man Mara's parents forced her to marry at a tender age, is shockingly brutal, consumed by this one passion of making a fortune in the city and later in Europe. He is prepared to sacrifice not only his own pride, but also everything of value, his family's heirloom, and then of course his wife, in the pursuit of his tragic delusion, his dream/doom. We cannot blame him enough for the series of humiliations and brutal treatments he inflicts on Mara, for instance forcing her to live with his new German wife as a "sister" and a house maid, ultimately driving her into prostitution so that he can live off the "profit". Even the fact that his dream eventually explodes into a nightmare and tosses him into jail does not offer any resolution to Mara's shame and misery. On the other hand, Mara's own lie of making her people back home in Ghana believe that she is making it good in Europe working in an African restaurant, cannot redeem her from the life of shame and abuse she is condemned to at Ove's brothel, "a lone, isolated house on the outskirts of Munich". She is unable to recognize herself in the mirror, as she stares painfully at "this bit of garbage

10

that once used to be (me)". Back home in Ghana, her family buys her lie and gains society's admiration on account of the money and other things she regularly sends home. One wonders what her mother and the rest of her family, or even society, would say if the truth of her condition were to be revealed to them. We shudder to think that they probably wouldn't, couldn't care. Not for her.

Perhaps we cannot altogether spare Mara herself part of the blame. If only she had listened to the timely and motherly advice offered her by Mama Koisk, to forget about Akobi, who on the eve of his departure for Germany, chooses to spend his last night with another woman, and does his best to stop Mara from seeing him off at the airport:

> To tell you the truth, Greenhorn, if I was you, now that he is gone I would forget him and start thinking wholly about yourself and your son. That is what you must do. These our men they always leave for Europe and say they'll be back in one or two or three years. "I am only going there to work and make money and return" is what they all say, but they go and they never return again. You must forget him. (pp. 45-46).

Somehow, Mara ignores probably the most important piece of advice anyone has offered her so far. We may also want to blame Mara for her lack of moral courage to find her way back home out of her life of misery. But will society and family welcome her back? Will they admit their own blame and compensate her with just a little bit of sympathy, if not apology? Something in the portrait of family and society painted here tells us that Mara may very well return to a life of scorn at home. This is where the real tragedy of this tale lies. She is trapped. Mara is trapped between Akobi's utterly selfish life of brutal greed and delusion, and her society/family's equally selfish and misguided expectations about a so-called good life in the city, their tragic illusions about the pleasures of life beyond the horizon in the white man's land.

It is important that we are not misled by the title of Amma Darko's second novel, *The Housemaid*, into unduly focusing critical attention on the girl Efia, the housemaid in the story. Indeed, it is doubtful whether we should regard her as the true *"central character"* of this novel. In fact, she does not even properly enter the story until we are almost half way through the narration. For me, part of the magic of this novel is that, slender as it is, it succeeds in rolling several individual life stories into one connected tale of multiple social and psychological implications. It is as much the life story of Akua, the street girl, as it is that of her much "luckier" friend Efia, who at least has a roof over her head and the "loving care" of her Madam, Tika. And it is also the life story of the "two boy scavengers searching the rubbish dump as usual for anything that might be useful" (p.5), only to stumble upon the red plastic bag of clothes "stained with plenty of blood and other fluids". Above all, *The Housemaid* is also the story of several elders who should have been there for these children, as responsible parents to these various children abandoned to their fate. It is the story of Efia's father, who "rinses his mouth with (akpeteshi) first thing every morning", was already fast asleep before noon on the day his daughter's fate was decided by the rest of the family, but woke up just in time to ask: "So what is in it for *us*?" Afia's mother is justifiably shocked at her husband's selfish and irresponsible reaction to their daughter's fate, but she too readily throws herself into the narrative as a willing accomplice to her own mother's diabolical plot to turn Efia's misery into a profitable family enterprise.

Mami Korkor, fresh fish hawker and mother of one of the "two scavenger boys", laments over her daughter Bibio "growing up on the wrong side of the tracks", but Bibio's life story, like those of her three siblings, is inevitably entangled with that of Mami Korkor herself. She could put the blame on the irresponsible man who "helped" her bring the children into a ruthless, uncaring world. But she must first answer ten-year old Bibio's painful question:

> Why, after making Nereley with him, when you realised how irresponsible he was, did you go ahead to make Akai, me and Nii Boi as well? (p. 11).

Perhaps the most damning of all the life stories that make up this one tragic tale are those of Tika and her mother Sekyiwa. And it is no accident that probably half the narrative evolves around these two characters, especially Tika, their dreams of material wealth, and the tragic collapse of those dreams into nightmares. These are two lives located on the far side of deprivation, but they are also among the least happy.

As readers, we are left to work out for ourselves the moral of all these life stories told as one brief, disturbing tale. That moral is probably located closer to the empty space between Sekyiwa and her daughter Tika: true happiness in life cannot be bought with cash, nor can it be secure by heartlessly sacrificing even those closest to us for personal gain. The final paragraph seems to suggest that Tika, helped by Teacher, has learned this ultimate lesson of life, and is ready to reach out for her mother, Sekyiwa, now abandoned by wealth and society:

> And she burst out laughing and crying at the same time. Teacher joined in. And, together, they laughed and cried; laughing and crying away their pain, their disappointment, their anger, their fear. And laughing with hope.

That final sentence, "And laughing with hope", may have been meant to take some of the poison out of a deadly tale. But with the specter of "the gruesome decaying corpse of a newborn baby girl" hanging over a bewildered society, it is doubtful whether merely "laughing with hope" is enough to free this community from the burden of its accumulated guilt. The community is not even ready to face its own guilt. Everyone is still too busy pointing fingers, shifting the blame on so-called witches and even the gods, too busy performing "the necessary rituals…to clear the curse" (p.103).

Beyond the Horizon concludes with the following statements by Mara: "Material things are all I can offer them. As for myself, there's nothing dignified and decent left for me to give them". The concluding reflections of *The Housemaid,* as seen in the dialogue between Teacher and Tika, seem to suggest that it should take much more than material wealth for individuals and communities to regain their hold on life. Somehow, we cannot but recall the earlier exchange between Sekyiwa and Tika, then a mere child longing for the warmth of parental care:

> 'Who will play with me on Saturdays if you can't take me to the shop?'
> 'I will find somebody.'
> 'Why can't you play with me?'
> 'Because I have to make money.'
> 'So when you finish making money, will you play with me?'
> But before Sekyiwa could answer that, she was summoned to talk to the new house-help she wanted to employ to look after Tika. Little Tika continued to wait and hope for the day her mother would finish making money and come to play with her (p. 20).

Significantly, it is on this note of an innocent child's constant yearning for the warmth of parental care that Amma Darko's new novel opens. Little Tika's hope in *The Housemaid* becomes Fofo's dream in *Faceless,* the dream with which we are led into the nightmare world of *Faceless.* Much later in the story, Fofo tells us that bad dreams are a normality with her: she is always sure to have "the nightmare of a good dream." Little Tika's dream is also the dream of those two other children abandoned, like Fofo, to the streets:

> "My dream," began the boy, "is to be able to go home one day to visit my mother and see a look of joy in her face at the sight of me. I want to be able to sleep beside her. I wish her to tell me she was happy I came to visit her.... She is always in a hurry to see my back. Sometimes I cannot help thinking that maybe she never has a smile for me because the man she made me with that is my father probably also never had a smile for her too."

Young as this boy is, he is able to locate the real burden of his life at its proper source: the absence of a responsible and caring husband and father from what could have been their home. He sympathizes with his mother, in spite of himself, in spite of his mother's shocking farewell to him: "Go. You do not belong here".

In *Faceless*, as in *The Housemaid*, we find the children thinking and speaking and acting above their age. This should not surprise us. Having been abandoned to the streets, each one of them has had to grow too quickly into the ways of the world in order take up for themselves those responsibilities their parents have turned their backs on. For many of these children, thinking, talking, and indeed acting "grown up" is a necessary skill for survival in a ruthless world:

> A part of Fofo was and would always be the fourteen years that she was; but the harshness of life on the streets had also made a premature adult of part of her. She was both a child and an adult and could act like both; talk like both; think like both and feel like both. What she wanted to do was to say a whole lot of things to hurt Maa Tsuru, and cause her pain:
> "I know Fofo. I know. Oh God!"
> "Don't bring in God's name, mother. You knew what you were doing when you chose him over . . ."

Maa Tsuru choked on saliva and coughed violently. "I don't have the strength to fight you with words Fofo," she spoke slowly, "And even if I did, I wouldn't do it."

In this confrontation between mother and daughter, we witness a terrifying reversal of the natural order of things. Not only has daughter's voice taken over with words of unassailable moral authority; her mother is forced, obviously by her own sense of guilt, to forfeit even the right to self-defense.

Even with the few lucky children with the security of a home, such as Kabria's three children, the things that come out of their "infant" mouths constantly startle us. Take for instance, Essie's philosophical exchange with her mother:

> And in response, Essie would be at her dreamer best: "Mum, you see? That is why I said you worry too much. Tomorrow hasn't even come yet, and already you are worrying about it. See?"

Essie's little brother Ottu is no less interesting/intriguing in his exchanges with his mother. Regrettably, not much sense comes out of the mouth of their father, Adade. In fact, each time he opens his mouth, we are afraid he is going to say something quite silly, quite selfish, or plain boring. Adade may not be our typical irresponsible husband or father, but he clearly does not measure up to anything close to a role model. As a father and especially as a husband, he seems to perform some of his responsibilities rather reluctantly, often grudgingly.

In the context of this novel, however, Adade is not too bad after all. At least, he does not abandon his family. And for this, his children and even their mother, can count themselves among the lucky few. As Kabria herself puts it: "The poor man was definitely other things. But foolish and irresponsible? No! That he definitely wasn't." Most certainly, their children are not condemned to "the devouring jaws of the streets," nor to the lurking danger of other men with devilish intentions towards vulnerable children, such as the wily rapist Onco pretending to be every child's Uncle, the bully Macho, or "the no-nonsense streetlord" appropriately named Poison.

Perhaps the most frightening lesson in *Faceless* is the fact that having lost their moral authority over their children, parents like Maa Tsuru are totally paralyzed by fear, the fear of terrors such as Poison. And it is left to the children to devise their own means of facing up to the Machos and Poisons of their world. There are those like Baby T who are destined to die the most agonizing kind of death. The only hope left is to be found in the unusual courage and intelligence of others such as Fofo. But the situation is so bad that even such courage and intelligence are not enough. Fofo still needs the kind of helping hand offered by Kabria and her colleagues at MUTE, the all-female NGO dedicated to helping to dig out the many buried voices of the dispossessed. And for all their brave effort, even the collective determination of the women of MUTE cannot face the challenge alone. They in turn need the intervention of an understanding media, through which the groans of the voiceless may be broadcast to an unbelieving world. The problem of street children has grown beyond any one individual or organization. It requires collaboration of the kind we find here between the women of MUTE and the radio presenter on Harvest FM, Sylv Po, to help save the situation.

Fofo in her innocence, insists she wants to see Government; she cannot think of anyone in her world to take up their case, especially the case of her sister Baby T. What she doesn't know is that Government itself has lost its priorities, its sense of direction; it has become dysfunctional and deaf to the cries of children abandoned or sold to the merciless streetlords of the Poison kind, and their equally heartless female collaborators such as Maami Broni.

Nothing can be more illustrative of Government's own paralysis than the state of complete helplessness and hopelessness in which we find the police station charged with the investigation of Baby T's murder. Like Vickie and Kabria, we are outraged by the surly police officer who welcomes us and especially by the inspector who is too busy checking his lotto numbers to notice our arrival. But our initial anger soon turns into embarrassment and even sympathy as the inspector takes us through a stock-taking of their "resources" for combating crime and maintaining peace: "Broken windows; leaking sewerages; cracked walls and peeled painting" ... the confidential filing cabinet with "a handle missing ... and a gaping hole where a lock should have been" ... "the single chair with the leather covering all torn-up"... but above all, the telephone ["It's dead", whimpered Kabria], and of course the empty yard with NOTHING in it, no vehicle, "not even a battered Tico!" So when the inspector finally turns round and asks, rather triumphantly: "And now, if I may ask again, what was it you said I should do for you?", what else can we say but join Kabria and Vickie in sad chorus: "Nothing."

There is enough here to make us give up hope for ourselves and for the children, like so many who are trapped in the overwhelming sadness of this tale — the countless children lost to the terrors of the street, the police inspector, his surly assistant, or Maa Tsuru and especially the man who should have been husband to her and father to her children, Kwei, who one day simply and completely "disappeared from their lives". Somehow, Amma Darko's vision of social reality would not allow our world to be completely swallowed up in such total gloom. Through the narrative technique of encircling Baby T's tragic end with Fofo's ultimate triumph, we are offered some hope, however fragile. And by inserting the somewhat happier, even comic story of Kabria's family into the desolate tale of Maa Tsuru and her children, Amma Darko provides us with a workable alternative to the completely dysfunctional family unit. Not that all is well with Kabria and her children and her husband, but at least the children are in school, the parents are at work, and together, they can sit down for meals as a family. And there is room in this family for even Creamy, her old and battered car, to be accepted as a full and useful member.

In-between the heavy burden of so many episodes, there is often hilarious dialogue and light-hearted comment to force us into laughter in spite of ourselves. We have already cited the state of the police station, deftly sketched out in tragi-comic characterization and hilarious dialogue. The use of the device of a mystery waiting to be solved, deriving largely from Baby T's gruesome death and the attempt to hide her true identity by completely defacing her beyond recognition, provides an intriguing impetus to the dedicated task force of the women from MUTE who take on the detective work of an inoperative police force. There may not be many likeable characters in this story, but almost all of them are portrayed with such traits as make them unforgettable. The portrait of Naa Yomo is an outstanding case in point. Our initial impression of her as a character with a nuisance value quickly gives way to amusement, and ultimately respect. For the women of MUTE, dedicated as they are to seeking hidden, even buried information, this 87-year old woman is something of a gold mine. And like a typical gold mine, hers is to provide a ton of information, leaving them to rummage though it for the occasional gem buried in a pile of rubbish.

The phenomenon of street children has become one of the most widely discussed social tragedies of our time. We are witnesses to a deluge of talk about the plight of these children, from newspaper articles, to radio talk-shows, television documentaries and elegant academic discussions. There are countless NGOs supposedly working for the interest of street children. Many well-funded, well-attended workshops and conferences have been convened on the subject. Even Government claims to be doing its very best to tackle the problem. And yet, in spite of all these well-publicized efforts, the problem not only persists but also seems to be getting even more intractable.

It is for this reason that Amma Darko's *Faceless* must be compulsory reading for all those who claim to be interested in the plight of street children. In this relatively short novel, street children cease to be mere statistics or a point of reference for media hysteria, academic discourse or political rhetoric. What do we tell the one street child who steps off the pages of this book and declares that she *knows* poverty, that she has in fact *seen* it? And what do we say or do as "normal people" the next time we wake up and find the mutilated corpse of yet another "unidentified/unidentifiable" child lying behind our house? Perhaps dismiss it as that of a *kayayoo*, may be that of "a girl of the street"? File away the post-mortem report in a broken police "confidential" filing cabinet, and eventually haul the unclaimed body away for burial in a mass grave at Mile Eleven? Can we possibly go back to peaceful sleep when it is all over? And will it ever be over? Before we head towards our bed, may be we should find out from Maami Broni what it is like to have the blood of just one street child on your hands:

> Not once since it happened have I known peace or sleep. When I am bathing, I am afraid to close my eyes! I see her everywhere. I hear sounds. I feel her unseen presence ... hearing the sounds in my head and feeling the weight of Baby T's spirit . . . I could have prayed to God for help but how dared I? . . . Her spirit is seated inside my head like a chief in state.

Like Maami Broni, our society will never know peace until we pay the full price for the children we have abandoned, until we learn to do the right thing by those others we hope to bring into our lives. And beyond the children, our society must also learn to do right by the class of socially and economically disadvantaged people "produced" by our various failed development programmes, and too often condemned to a nightmarish existence in those sections of our urban centres systematically "overlooked" by our planners of urban growth. The media have given us their views on the city of Accra's own incarnation of the biblical Sodom and Gomorrah, growing like a dangerous boil in the city's nerve centre. But it is a view based very much on security reports compiled by a frustrated police force to suit the biases of a negligent society. Amma Darko's *Faceless*, is as much a story of children abandoned to the streets as it is that of our various Sodom and Gomorrahs, whole communities abandoned to their fate by a self-satisfied and discriminatory machinery of state.

In Amma Darko's *Beyond the Horizon*, *The Housemaid*, and especially *Faceless*, there is a wake-up call to us as Grandmothers/ Grandfathers, as Mothers, but especially as Fathers. It is not enough to sow the seeds of human life in quick, repeated sessions of reckless ecstasy. Beyond the delight of tears, beyond the passionate intensity of countless orgasms, the future of our children, of our own mortality and ancestry awaits our constant vigilance and careful nurturing. No seed grows into harvest joys without the planter's diligent labour of love. Until we come to this understanding as parents, as family, as community, we will forever stand condemned by the anguish in the eyes and the voices of our children, forever guilty of "the nurturing of ... prospective soul(s) into the devouring jaws of the streets".

Swarthmore, Pennsylvania
January 12, 2003

BOOK ONE

1

[handwritten annotation: really poor area]

S he chose to spend the night on the old cardboard laid out in front of the provision store at the Agbogbloshie market place because it was a Sunday. It had nothing to do with Sunday being a church going day. The reason was simply that if she hadn't, she would have stood the risk of losing her newly acquired job of washing carrots at the vegetables wholesale market. Fofo would have spent the Sunday night into Monday dawn with her friends across the road at the squatters enclave of Sodom and Gomorrah watching adult films her fourteen years required her to stay away from, and drinking directly from bottles of *akpeteshie,* or at best, some slightly milder locally produced gin. Ultimately she would have found herself waking up Monday morning beside one of her age group friends, both of them naked, hazy and disconcerted; and oblivious to what time during the night they had stripped off their clothes and what exactly they had done with their nakedness. Sucked into life on the streets and reaching out to each new day with an ever-increasing hopelessness, such were the ways they employed to escape their pain.

A boy and a girl of about Fofo's age and making a home on the streets of Accra like her were once asked by a reporter from one of the private FM stations during a survey about their most passionate dreams. Dreams as in Martin Luther King's famous words: "I have a dream." The reporter thought the kids would be craving for material things like shoes and dresses or more practically, blankets for warmth at night. She was swerved. They craved for warmth all right, but of a kind that many with secure roofs over their heads and the assured love of a parent, at least, took for granted.

"My dream," began the boy, "is to be able to go home one day to visit my mother and see a look of joy on her face at the sight of me. I want to be able to sleep beside her. I wish her to tell me she was happy I came to visit her. Whenever I visit her, she doesn't let me stay long before she asks me politely to leave. She never has a smile for me. She is always in a hurry to see my back. Sometimes I cannot help thinking that maybe she never has a smile for me because the man she made me with that is my father probably also never had a smile for her too. One day she said to me, 'Go. You do not belong here.' If I don't belong to where she is, where do I belong? But I know that it is not just that she doesn't want to see me. She worries about the food that she has. It is never enough. So she worries that it may not suffice for her two new children if I joined. The ones she has with the man who is their father and who is her new husband. He hates to see my face. I often wonder what it is I remind him of so much."

The girl said, "One day a kind woman I met at a centre made me very happy. Before I went there, I knew that by all means she would give me food. But this woman gave me more. She hugged me. I was dirty. I smelled bad. But she hugged me. That night I slept well. I had a good dream. Sometimes I wish to be hugged even if I am smelling of the streets."

It was around 2 a.m. and Fofo, though not being hugged, was smiling in her sleep. Not that she was aware of it herself. But God above and the angel watching over her saw the smile and knew it was the smile of a contented fourteen-year-old girl who, but for the life that fate had plunged her into, should have been smiling that way each night in her sleep. Fofo was smiling because she was having a dream that was far removed from the realities of the life she lived. It was a dream as in the group of thoughts and images experienced during sleep. And in her dreams, she was living in a home with a roof. She was there when it suddenly began

26

to rain and she was going to rush to somewhere in search of a safe and dry place to huddle close to other kids for warmth when it dawned on her that she had a roof over the head. And in the home with a roof, there was a toilet. A toilet with a roof. She smiled so wide when she felt the urge to attend to nature's call that the angel watching over her smiled too. In the dream, she simply entered the toilet with a roof and did her thing. No war like it many times was when she had to do it in real life. The bullies, mostly the older and more seasoned street boys, and their thick-set leader, Macho, also regularly unloaded the solid waste contents of their bowels onto the rubbish dumps and in the gutters and open drainages. Then after freeing themselves, they would begin to yell out how very determined they were to keep the environment clean and go after the likes of her to line their pockets, under the guise of 'spot fine', with whatever money she had begged for or stolen or earned the previous day.

She was smiling still in her dream and doing it comfortably in the toilet with a roof when she felt the light pressure on her breasts under the weight of a pair of hands that were definitely not the Lord's. The hands began to play around her bosom. Slowly she began her descent from dream to reality. She felt a squeeze, which jolted her very rudely into full awakenment. She opened her eyes slightly. Someone was kneeling over her. She opened the eyes a little. It was a man. She stiffened, closed the eyes again and remained still. Instincts guided. The hand travelled gradually and purposefully down to her stomach. Her heart pounded violently, threatening to explode inside her chest. The hand moved further down. Instinct continued to guide. She opened her eyes again. Wider. Two viscious eyes glared back at her under the illumination of the storefront bulb. She stared into the face above her. Was her mind playing games with her? She looked again. It was the no-nonsense streetlord, Poison of the streets, all right. A man who used to be the leader of the bullies like Macho now was. Who used to be content with just 'spot fines', but whose eyes, like they say, opened, somewhere along the line and caused him to fight his way to his present position of 'street lord'. Fofo let out a cry and began to kick her hands and legs wildly in the air. One huge muscular hand came down hard upon her mouth and suppressed the sounds from her throat. The other restrained her flailing hands and legs. The angel still looking on shed a tear. Poison successfully captured her legs between his kneeling thighs.

"You want to live?" He hissed.

Fofo moaned and nodded under the gravity of his hands.

"Then no noise!" He warned.

Fofo thought fast and wild. Her guts led her on. Then fate preached her the gospel according to street wisdom. She ceased her weak grappling, sighed heavily and went limp. Poison grinned like the devil himself. The confidence of a fool. The folly of evil. Fofo lay there like a defeated soul. Poison pushed up her dress and scowled at the sight of her underpants. He muttered an obscenity and yanked it off. Fofo surrendered to her instincts. Poison unbuckled his belt. Then the angel descended. And it was so swift and so sudden that even Fofo herself didn't see it coming. It was an instant reaction of reflexes that in the split of that second responded to a stimulus without soliciting the involvement of the brain. Her right leg struck at flesh. Her left leg kicked into muscle. Her fists bashed and banged into facial organs, hitting into both softness and bones. By the time sanity returned, the big muscular frame of Poison was swaying above her, one hand clutching the groin, the other shielding an obviously wounded eye. His face was contorted and oozing pure pain. Fofo shot up and grabbed the black plastic bag beside her. She cast one last look at the groaning mass on the ground, gave up on her underpants and bolted like the devil was at her heels.

Odarley, Fofo's friend, was fast asleep when she felt the tap on her arm; gently at first, then harshly. She groaned and half opened her eyes with reluctance. Her head was pounding from the previous day's drinking spree. She ran a hand over her belly and below. She still had her pants on. It was fairly illuminated inside the wooden shack because the door was never shut. It had no windows and they would all have sweated and suffocated to death if the door was ever shut. Paying two hundred cedis a day each to the owner, it was what they could afford. There were the regulars like herself and until a week ago, Fofo. The owner was never short of his daily tenants. Boys and girls slept together, stripped together and did things with each other, many times under the influence of alchohol, wholly unconscious of what they were doing or with whom. Such was the evil of life on the streets. She looked to her left. The shoe shine boy who had come so strong on to her the previous night at the video centre was still fast asleep and stark naked. The iced water seller to his left was also completely naked. Odarley put two and two together and it made sense then why she still had her pants on. In their drunken stupor, the shoeshine boy mistook the iced water girl for her. She turned attention back to the apparition that patted her on the arm and opened her eyes full. They widened at the sight of her friend.

"Fofo, is that you? What are you . . .?"

"Shshshshshsh . . ." Fofo placed a finger to her own lips.

Odarley shot up from the cardboard and rubbed her eyes. A car horn sounded afar like a clarion call to duty. She rose.

Fofo made her way carefully out of the shack. Odarley followed, pausing briefly by the door to fish out her *Charlie wotee* from a bunch. She slipped in her feet and stepped out with Fofo. On second thought, she got back inside the shack. A big plastic water bottle stood by the pile of slippers. She picked an old plastic cup beside it and filled it with some of the water. She walked out to the crudely dug gutter in front of the shack, washed her face and rinsed her mouth.

"Have you?" she asked Fofo.

Fofo shook her head.

Odarley handed her the half-cup of water and went back into

the shack. By the time Fofo returned the cup, Odarley had fished out some chewing sticks. She placed one between her teeth; gave the other to Fofo; chewed briefly on hers; removed it, spat into the gutter and whispered, "Trouble?"

"Big one."

Odarley's mind went ablaze with what Fofo's big trouble most likely was. Maybe the vegetables woman who employed her found out Fofo sometimes picked pockets. Or had Fofo tried a fast one on somebody and failed?

"What big trouble?" she asked, "And what trouble here at Sodom and Gomorrah isn't big? I tell you, how we boozed yesterday? That one was big trouble. Nature is even calling." She held her stomach. "Let's go to the dump." And went ahead.

A handful of children and a few adults were already there and doing their own thing under the scrutinizing eyes of some early rising pigs and vultures. They found a free spot. Odarley raised her dress and pulled down her pants and got straight to business. Fofo also lifted her dress and squatted. Odarley who was observing her, shot out, "You are wearing no underpant?"

"You let us finish fast and get out of here before Macho comes. You know how he has been harassing people nowadays, don't you?" Fofo responded.

They were facing each other like two alternate angels. It enabled them to watch each other's back.

"Honestly," Odarley snorted, "Macho himself, where does he do it? He is a foolish man. Where does he want us to do it?"

"He wants us to go to the public toilet up there. Where else?"

"Nonsense. Then why doesn't he and his gang also go there? Who can walk that long distance to up there when the thing is coming with force?"

"Ask again. And look at the long line of people too always there. Ah! Even if you go there at twelve midnight, you would find a queue."

"That is why people sometimes do it on themselves while waiting for their turn. This is not like hunger where you can force small and say like: oh, let me hold on a little. This one, when it says it is a coming, zoom! It comes. Bum! Like that! What does it understand about holding on a little?"

"And see how sometimes too when you are in there doing it and haven't finished at all, those guard people too would come on you telling you to hurry up because you have kept too long and others are waiting. Is this something that you can start doing and stop midway just because you have kept long and others too are waiting?"

"Hm."

Odarley seemed to be concentrating. She groaned a little.

Fofo was obviously having a problem. "Odarley, do you think God is watching us do it?"

"Ah, don't they say He sees everything? But why this question? You squat there and ask foolish questions. Me, I am about to finish."

"What? Just now?"

"You call all the time we have been here, just now? Do you want Macho to come after you with those thick round arms of his like Mami Adzorkor's kenkey balls?"

Fofo didn't reply.

"Fofo," Odarley called.

"Hm."

"I am about to finish oh."

Fofo didn't respond.

"Are you also about to finish?"

"No."

"No? Why?"

"Ah, me do I know why? It's refusing to come."

"Oho! What did you eat yesterday?"

"Yesterday, what time?"

"Yesterday morning. What did you eat?"

"Bread. Tea bread."

31

"And in the afternoon?"

"Bread. Sugar bread."

"*Ebei!* And in the evening? Don't even answer. I am sure it was some of Kwansima Fante's butter bread. No?"

"Yes."

"Hm. You ate bread, bread, bread like that? With what?"

"Water. Yesterday was a bad day."

"Then give up and let's go. Don't you know that you end up cheating your own self when you try to cheat the spider? By now the plenty bread has turned to concrete inside your stomach. Let's go!" And rustled her piece of old newspaper.

Fofo panicked and groaned aloud.

"Eh, are you forcing?"

"But what should I do?"

"You will get piles oh!" she rose.

"Don't go and leave me, please!"

"I am waiting; but you are keeping too long. Do you hear the lorry engines revving? Macho would be here any . . ."

"Everybody s-c-a-tt-e-r-r-r-r- . . . oh! He is coming oh!" Someone yelled.

Everybody and everything within sight went hey-y; even the pigs and vultures.

Odarley was yards away before Fofo could even make it to her feet. By which time Macho's glistening baldhead was already within sight. Fofo bolted.

"You've left your plastic bag!" Odarley screamed, "Look! He has taken it!"

Fofo turned. She had completely forgotten the bag.

Macho looked inside it and grinned.

"He's got all of my money from last week." Fofo whined.

"All of it?"

"All of it." And broke down in tears.

"So what are you going to do now?"

Fofo didn't hesitate. "I am going to see my mother."

"For money?"

"Am I a dreamer? She and me who needs money more?"

"Then what are you going to see her about?"

"The big trouble I told you about."

"The big trouble?"

"Yes. Poison."

"Poison? The Poison? The street lord?"

Fofo nodded.

Odarley grew scared. "Why on earth should you become involved with him?"

"I didn't. The person I said tried to rape me, that was him."

Odarley laughed. Her initial scare turned to bemusement. "Oh Fofo! Who would believe you? Poison doesn't go raping girls like us. He doesn't need to. When he wants it, he beckons, and the hi-life girls flood to him in their numbers. Are you sure of what you are saying?"

"Yes. But I don't know why. I don't understand it either. That is why I want to see my mother. She has some connection with him. I don't know exactly what. But I know she knows him."

"Who doesn't?"

"I mean … she knows him more."

"How? How do you know?"

"I heard her and my stepfather talk once. That was before I quit home. And they mentioned Poison more than once."

"Were they fighting?"

"No. It was a conversation. A conversation and an argument in one."

"And you never told me?"

"I never thought much of it. But now that Poison tried to . . ."

"Fofo, are you sure it was him?"

"It was he."

2

Fate's machinery got into motion elsewhere that same Monday dawn and placed on a string two destinies joined carefully at their seams by an unclear thread. Like a shadow crossing paths at the bidding of death's uncanny ways, Kabria, in the comfort of her modest home in a middle class suburb of Accra, remembered that her regular garden eggs and tomatoes vendors at the Agbogbloshie market would be expecting her.

The mother of three children between the ages of seven and fifteen, events both in and outside the home sometimes got her thinking that those ought to be the most impossible of all ages.

Married sixteen years to Adade, her architect husband, Kabria passionately loved her job with MUTE, a Non Governmental Organisation that was basically into documentation and information build up. And with equal fervour, she loathed the figure that appeared on her monthly salary slip. But topping it all was her shamelessness about her special attachment to her old-hand-me-down-thank-you-very-much-Adade 1975 VW Beetle nicknamed Creamy.

The mother, wife, worker and battered car owner that she was, no day passed that Kabria didn't wonder how come the good Lord created a day to be made up of only twenty four hours, because from dawn to dusk, domestic schedules gobbled her up; office duties ate her alive; her three children devoured her with their sometimes realistic and many times very unrealistic demands; while the icing on the cake, their father, needed do no more than simply be your regular husband, and she was in a perpetual quandary.

Obea, her first child, at fifteen, had reached so to say, that age. Three years after her grand entry into the teen world, three to qualifying to vote. And as much as Kabria could recall, Obea said goodnight to her one night, baby faced, flat chested and all, only to wake up the following morning sporting a blossoming bosom and a pair of fairly rounded hips. The result? Obea threw both Kabria and Adade into absolute turmoil. There she was, one minute their little girl, next moment protesting any reference to her as their little girl. And while Kabria suffered her period of discomfort in silence, praying to God for guidance on how to deal with her now physically maturing daughter, Adade for his part, retired to bed each night wondering if the time had not come for him to maybe invest in two bulldogs to discourage potential young male whistlers behind the wall.

Her second child, Essie, was nine and the source of a different kind of worry to Kabria.

Essie was born at midnight. Kabria ignored the age-old superstition that alleged midnight borns grew up with their feet everywhere else but firmly on the ground. She should otherwise have performed a rite like touching Essie's tiny feet three times on hot sand, three days following her birth, to nullify the dreamer jinx. Nine years on, and she couldn't help but wonder at times if maybe; just maybe, she should not have underestimated that notion after all. Especially when it came to some of the methods and timings of Essie's financial and material demands. This normally followed a certain peculiar pattern.

"Mum," she would begin, "You worry too much. Do you know that you worry too much? It's not good for you, don't you see?"

As though Kabria herself thought of worrying as an essential vitamin. As though she deemed it to be good for her soul. As though she worried just for the sake of worrying instead of like in a situation of finding herself counting and recounting the money in her purse with the deepest of frowns and cancelling out items on the household shopping list; sort of doing the financial balancing act; none of which Essie would take note of.

"Money is for spending, Mum, you know," she would go on, like a crooked preacher from a disoriented pulpit, "We came to meet it. We will leave it behind."

Then drop the surprise. Something like, "But if you like, I will hold on with my blouse till tomorrow."

"Blouse? What blouse?" Kabria would yell between the desire to shove a piece of cloth inside Essie's mouth and her maternal urge to exercise control and be patient even in the face of such an outrageous and inconsiderate provocation from no less a person than one of the three in her life to whom she had rented out her womb free of charge for a whole nine months. Not one single month's rent charged.

"It's a tube top." Essie would reply gingerly, as though just descended from another planet.

"Tube top? Didn't you just see me count and recount the money in my purse?"

And an unperturbed Essie would say calmly, "That is why I said I would hold on till tomorrow."

"That was why you said? Who said I would have the money for it tomorrow? Where would it spring from?"

And in response, Essie would be at her dreamer best. "Mum, you see? That is why I said you worry too much. Tomorrow hasn't even come yet, and already you are worrying about it. See?"

Her last child, Ottu, was their only son. And what an attitude Ottu carried upon his little shoulders for being an only boy. It was as though seven years ago, the good Lord above had summoned Ottu's then asexual soul, announced His intention to clothe him in flesh and dispatch him down to earth via Kabria's womb and so gave him the option to choose the preferable sex Ottu would want to be on earth. Ottu chose to come as a male, only to realize upon his descent into Kabria's life that indeed he had done her a big favour with his decision to the good Lord, because she had two daughters already and was desperate for a son; and he always held Kabria to ransom whenever a situation sort of demanded it. For example when he lost his school lunchbox for the second time in a term and Kabria decided to act tough and decreed that she was going to make him go to school for one whole week with his lunch packed in a black polythene bag, his reaction was not kind either.

"Mum, do you know that I cut short your problems by coming as a boy and earned you respect?" Ottu claimed unexpectedly.

Kabria was so taken aback by it that she found herself asking, "What problems?"

"I have a friend at school," Ottu launched into a self promotion campaign, "They are six ... "

"Six children?"

"Yes."

"In this day and age?"

"That is why my friend is special."

And Kabria wondered where this was leading. "Ottu, please, every child is special. Every child ought to be precious to the parents, be they even ten or twenty."

"Mum, you don't understand," Ottu reproached, "he is also the only son. Just like me. And his grandmother said he is special. Veeeeeery special."

Kabria began to suspect where the conversation was leading to and asked carefully, "Did he say why his grandmother said that?"

"Yes. You see, by coming as a boy, he earned his mother plenty of respect and also ended her pains."

"Her pains?'

"Yes. When you are bringing forth a baby, they say it is painful. Veeeeeery painful. No?"

Kabria very stubbornly ignored that. Her beloved son went on unperturbed anyway.

"You see, my friend's grandmother said that had my friend not come as a boy, she, being my friend's father's mother, would have insisted and ensured that my friend's mother continued to bear more and more children till she bore a son."

"Really?"

"Yes. And because of that, his Mum never punishes my friend. If you like when you take us to school tomorrow, I'll call him for you to ask him yourself."

Kabria turned down the offer with stiff politeness, told her son that like his two sisters, he too was special, but definitely not because he was a boy. And would have been equally special had he also come as a girl.

Next was Adade who always rose from bed each working day at 6 a.m. never one minute earlier. And which was a whole hour after Kabria. His expectation to find his breakfast table laid ready and waiting after he had hijacked the bathroom for thirty minutes and used up another fifteen minutes to dress up, was always met religiously by Kabria. He never came to the breakfast table without a newspaper in his hand. To Adade, that would be akin to wearing shoes without socks. So that, sometimes, he would rather re-read a newspaper he had already read, than not read at table at all. His motto was that, old news was better than no news. And if his head was buried in a newspaper, and Kabria asked a question, all she got was a nod or a shake of the head for an answer. Sometimes stubbornness and frustration pushed her on to persist till she got him to open the mouth. But the often brief and snappy reply was always never worth the energy she invested in her persistence.

After work, Adade normally met with friends at a drinking spot to socialize over bottles of beer. "To release tension," he would say. "Every man needs that to hold onto his sanity."

Kabria often wondered which of them needed a more urgent release of tension. Whether it shouldn't be she, who after having been labelled the weaker sex, had to, in spite of a full time job, perform all of her traditional duties at home, without an iota of relief. Every day after work, while Adade set off on route to go and release his tension, she had to go and pick up the children from school, head straight for home, change clothes, and go to the kitchen to see to dinner. Only to have him declare first thing on arrival home after releasing his tension, "Oh Kabria, I am so tired!"

Finally, Creamy. The car had been in and out of every kind of workshop from Abeka to Zongo so many times and undergone all kinds of clinical and plastic surgeries, that it seemed to have grown immune to both. Creamy; a name Kabria held so dear to heart that she once shocked Adade with the extent of her passion when he dared put it to the test.

It was after one of Creamy's many plastic surgeries, which left it, so tattooed that it required urgent re- spraying. Unable to squeeze anything out of her miserly salary, she sought help from Adade.

"Don't you receive a salary?" Adade asked.

"Don't get sarcastic with me." Kabria retorted, "If I had had the time to study further like you did, I would also have been reaping the benefits today in terms of a better salary. But I was busy making babies then. Remember?"

It was a line of argument Adade always tried to avoid. "Okay," he said simply to shut her up. But come the subsequent first day and second day and third day; and neither word nor assistance came. Kabria cast her mind onto the daily bottles of beers gobbled up in the name of releasing tension and paid Adade a surprise visit at his fine office the fourth day.

Tu-tu-tu-tu-tu . . . Creamy's furious engine and exhaust heralded its tattooed arrival. And Kabria, who meant business, parked it right beside Adade's brand new Toyota Corona, provided him on loan by his employers. When Adade saw his wife and her car, he prayed desperately for the earth to open up and swallow him whole. Kabria compounded his embarrassment by deliberately soliciting for more attention with her loud and gay hellos to all of Adade's co workers; then in their full and attentive glare, hopped gingerly into the car and drove away in the same tu-tu-tu-tu-tu fashion. Her little coup d'etat paid off. Adade came home that night with the required car paint.

"Is it cream?" Kabria asked.

Adade gave her a look to kill.

"What colour is it?" she pressed.

"Blue!" he snapped.

"Blue?" she roared.

"Yes. Metallic sea blue!"

"What kind of a bit and pieces colour is that?" she wailed.

Adade flared up; utterly flabbergasted. "Bits and pieces of a colour?"

"Yes." Kabria howled. "How do I call my Creamy, Creamy, after it has been sprayed this metallic sea blue?"

Adade was so shocked into a stupor he didn't know what to say. And was so furious that when he attempted to speak, it came out a wheeze. He returned the paint the following day, declined the offer to exchange it at a little inconvenience cost for a cream colour, and told Kabria bluntly that for all he cared, she could call at his office ten thousand times a day with her tattooed tu-tu-tu-tu Creamy.

After three weeks he gave in to her stubbornness and determination to drive Creamy in its tattooed state rather than have it sprayed any other colour than cream.

So, that was Kabria, the regular wife, mother, worker, and car owner, minding her own regular business until she took the decision that Monday morning to visit the Agbogbloshie market for some garden eggs and tomatoes.

3

Maa Tsuru, Fofo's mother, was leaning by her charred door sill. Her blank eyes, staring into nothingness, did not notice Odarley enter the compound house. Just a few years back, and Fofo could have been one of the numerous screaming children, scrambling with the sheep and goats and chickens for space to play and exist in the common compound. Fofo could have been the girl in the tattered brown underpants with the diseased red hair and a protruding stomach, carried on legs that were as thin as two dried sticks. Or the other in the flour sac underpant with a body ravaged by rashes and whose nose seemed to never stop running.

Maa Tsuru's extended family home was a house of many faces. And Odarley, there as, so to say, John the Baptist, took in all the hawk-like eyes that stole suspicious stares at her. She ventured past the first of the twelve rooms. That door and that of the second room were both shut. In front of the third, a girl of about eight was fanning a charcoal pot fire. Odarley greeted the girl's mother who was washing clothes in an aluminium basin. The woman didn't respond. Odarley greeted her again; louder. Again, the woman didn't respond. There was no way she could not have heard the second greeting.

"Mama," the eight year old girl called her mother, "She was greeting you." And pointed at Odarley.

The woman glared at her daughter. "Did I tell you I was deaf?" she roared.

The girl recoiled.

"Dare to imply that again and see how your cheeks will burn under the heat of my palms like the fire you are lighting."

"Mother I was only . . ."

"Shut up! Shut your big mouth up! If you like, open it again! Open it and see. I'll give you such a whack your head will do the *tselenke* by force. Foolish girl!"

"All because of one greeting?" Odarley was baffled. The woman knew her. That was obvious. And knew she was there to see Maa Tsuru. The woman's behavior therefore could only mean one thing. That she was at loggerheads with Maa Tsuru. Who else was? And why?

She walked on to the fifth room, ignoring the two young women plaiting their hair in front of the fourth. She didn't want to generate another war with a simple greeting.

In the midst of angry mothers and screaming children and bleating goats and sheep, Maa Tsuru looked like a soul drowned in torpidity. The baby in her arm didn't seem to even impact into her oblivion. And but for the sounds from the child's throat, her world was dead. A life dissolved in absolute lethargy. Odarley smiled sadly; then even that sad smile waned when she noticed the desperate scramble of one tiny hand to ferret for something almost non-existent in Maa Tsuru's bosom. The weak grab of the loose and hanging breast. The searching mouth in the tiny lean face. The voracious draw on the tired wrinkled nipple. The spurt of energy from the enervated body that was clearly the anger of a little hungry child. And Odarley knew that the gurgling of Fofo's half brother was one of anguish. In process, was the nurturing of another prospective soul into the devouring jaws of the streets. A life brought forth for the sake of bringing forth. A hungry mouth created not out of want.

"Maa Tsuru," Odarley called softly when she neared the door.

Fofo's mother turned her head and rested a glazed look on the face of her daughter's friend.

42

"I was coming with Fofo but she stopped on the way." Odarley divulged.

"Why?" Maa Tsuru asked in a voice that was hollow and inert.

"Because . . . she was uncertain . . . she wanted to come and see you about . . ."

"Hey!" an old voice croaked from the direction of the room almost opposite Maa Tsuru's, to the left, "Girl, are your manners gone on holidays? Have you heard of something called 'greeting' before?"

Odarley turned her head sharply to trade an insult, but mellowed immediately at the sight of the utterer. Naa Yomo at eighty-seven, was the oldest member of the household, and mother and grandmother and great grandmother to someone and everyone. If the washing woman did not appreciate her courtesy for whatever reason, Naa Yomo obviously expected it, for whatever reason. Odarley went over and greeted her politely. Naa Yomo responded and asked how she was doing.

"Fine, Naa Yomo."

"And your friend?"

"She is also fine, Naa Yomo."

"Didn't she come with you to see her mother?"

"She did, Naa Yomo. She is coming on the way. I took the lead but I'll go and call her to hurry up."

"Good. Good. And grandchild, tell her to greet me when she comes, will you?"

"I will Naa Yomo. I am sorry I didn't greet you earlier. It was because I didn't know what was happening. When I greeted the woman . . ."

"I know. I saw it all. It's all right. Go."

Maa Tsuru was submerged in sadness when Odarley returned to her. "I have become a leper in my own home," she muttered, more to herself than to Odarley and asked, "Why did you say Fofo stopped on the way?"

"Because something happened, Maa Tsuru." Odarley hushed.

Maa Tsuru became agitated. Her tepid disposition turned to one of alarm. She became suspicious of what could have happened and feared the suspicion.

"Do you know what . . ."

"Yes," Odarley cut her short, "Poison, Maa Tsuru. Poison."

It was no longer a suspicion to be wished away. "Oh God!" she cried from the darkest depths of fear, her sleeping emotions bursting forth. "Go and call her, Odarley. Hurry up. Go." And when Odarley turned and hurried away, cried once more to herself, "Oh God!"

The entire three hundred and sixty five days of the previous year, Fofo had visited the house not more than twice, even though her abode at Sodom and Gomorrah was only some few kilometers away. The current year was already into its fifth month, and but for the nightmare with Poison, she still would not have been calling. Her emotions about the woman who had carried her for nine full months in the womb confused her some times. Deep down inside her, she felt some affection for Maa Tsuru. Yet an overpowering urge to hate her also consumed her sometimes. She often pondered over whether what she deemed to be hatred was merely a desire to cushion the pain of her existence and to blame Maa Tsuru whom she held responsible for dumping her in the world. Because that was how she felt about herself. Dumped. But the thoughts of hatred for her mother sometimes scared her, for one could have only one natural mother in one's lifetime and there was already too much hatred out there on the streets. So when she thought of her sister, Baby T, and their stepfather, she often concluded that maybe, what she deemed to be hatred for her mother was actually a passionate loathing for some of the things Maa Tsuru had done. That maybe it was her intense hatred for those things that diminished to almost non-existence, the delicate line between her mother herself and the things she had done. They were thoughts that she sometimes wished desperately to go away. But something always awakened them like restless ghosts at night. Like now, when her eyes beheld the creaking wooden gate of the compound house.

Having been briefed by Odarley on the way, she greeted no one else aside Naa Yomo when she entered the house; then joined Odarley in front of the fifth room.

"Mother," she acknowledged Maa Tsuru without emotion.

"Fofo," Maa Tsuru responded with difficulty and asked immediately, "did he do something to you?"

Before Fofo replied, Maa Tsuru glanced across at Naa Yomo. The old lady had fixed a stare on them. Maa Tsuru grew nervous.

"Shall we go into the room?" She entered first. Fofo followed. Odarley remained outside.

The room was partitioned with an old translucent curtain. Fofo's four years old other half brother was asleep on a mat on the floor in the space in front of the curtain which served as the living room. Maa Tsuru raised and pegged one corner of the curtain onto the line and entered the inner space, which was the bedroom. She slumped onto the bed and waited. Fofo hesitated, then moved and sat down carefully at the farthest point from her mother. Life on the streets made mixed up persons out of children. She looked about the room and back at Maa Tsuru. Something did not quite fit. Then it dawned on her. What it was that didn't seem right. Something was missing.

"Where is he, mother?" she asked Maa Tsuru.

Maa Tsuru winced. She attempted to say something but her voice failed her. She paused, swallowed saliva and tried again.

"He left." She said simply.

"He left?" It was a wail of pain. "After all that he did to Baby T? To us all? He left? And you stood by and just allowed this smallish man to leave? Just like that?"

Tears welled up in Maa Tsuru's eyes. She did not speak. She couldn't.

"What made him leave, mother?" Fofo howled on, "And before he left, did you remind him of what you did for his sake? What you sacrificed? Did you?"

Maa Tsuru began to weep.

"I asked you, mother. Did you?"

Maa Tsuru began to cry. "Go away, Fofo," she managed between tears, "Go!"

Fofo's face clouded fiercely. "Is history repeating itself here? Are you sacking me, mother? Because of him?"

"No! No! I am not sacking you from here. Not from this room. Not from this house. I mean to say, go away. From Accra, if possible, Fofo. Go away. Go somewhere far away from here where he can never find you."

"What are you talking about, mother? Is it Poison? What does he want with me?"

"Oh, child!" Maa Tsuru sobbed, "Go away. Go."

"Why mother? Why?"

"Because they are animals. They know no mercy. And my hands are tied. Please. Go!"

A part of Fofo was and would always remain the fourteen years that she was; but the harshness of life on the streets had also made a premature adult of part of her. She was both a child and an adult and could act like both; talk like both; think like both and feel like both. What she wanted to do was to say a whole lot of things to hurt Maa Tsuru, and cause her pain. But she held back. Her mother was still not making complete sense.

"Why should I go away, mother? Who are they?"

Maa Tsuru wiped away her tears with the back of her hand and blew her nose into her cover cloth. "It's Baby T," she said eventually.

"Baby T?"

"Yes. Maami Broni . . ."

"The fat fair woman she lives with?"

"Yes. She came to me last week."

"So? Doesn't she sometimes come to . . ."

"I know Fofo. I know. Oh God!"

"Don't bring in God's name, mother. You knew what you were doing when you chose him over . . ."

"It was for their sake," she pointed at the baby and the sleeping boy, "what should I have done?"

"I don't know. But you should never have fed him and his sons at Baby T's expense. You don't see her. I don't see her. We don't know how she has grown to look like. All for what, mother? For what?"

Maa Tsuru didn't respond. She wiped away fresh tears from her face and resumed from where she had left off. "Something happened, Fofo."

"Something is always happening, no? Always. And had I not gotten the good sense to leave home, who knows, he probably would have made you send me away too to work for some woman to make money for you four to live on. No?"

Maa Tsuru choked on saliva and coughed violently. "I don't have the strength to fight you with words Fofo," she spoke slowly, "and even if I did, I wouldn't do it."

Fofo said nothing.

Maa Tsuru went on. "Last week a body was found behind a blue rasta hairdressing kiosk salon at Agbogbloshie. Did you hear about it?"

"Aren't bodies always being found there like the aborted fetuses at Sodom and Gomorrah? Is that news? Well, maybe for people like you living in proper homes like here, it is. No?"

Maa Tsuru ignored the sarcasm to avoid the bait of another round of war with words, for, what she was about to say, was in itself, war enough. "Maami Broni didn't come to give me money, Fofo. She came because she was afraid."

Fofo frowned. Her unasked question was obvious.

Maa Tsuru went on. "Since she was the one I entrusted Baby T to, she . . ."

"What are you trying to say, mother?"

". . . She came to tell me."

"Tell you what?"

"That the body behind the hairdressing salon . . ." fresh tears choked the rest of her words.

Fofo's eyes widened. "Baby T?"

Maa Tsuru began to shake.

Fofo just sat there and stared at her. She felt no immediate pain. Even the anger and mixed feelings lay low. In her mind's eye, all she saw was a recollection of the last time she ever laid eyes on her sister. Baby T's reddish and swollen eyes from too much crying, with her belongings tied up in an old headscarf and held loosely in her right hand as she followed Maami Broni out of the compound house.

Her calmness, when she opened her lips again to address Maa Tsuru, surprised her own self. "Mother, what is happening? Where do I fit into all this? What has all this got to do with Poison?"

"He got upset when he heard of Maami Broni's visit to me. He knew she had come to tell me."

"Tell you what? Are you saying Baby T is dead?"

Maa Tsuru nodded.

Fofo didn't know what to think. "So Baby T is dead?"

Maa Tsuru nodded again.

Fofo was scared and confused and in great emotional pain all at once. "My sister was staying with Maami Broni. Then she dies. So Maami Broni comes to inform you about it. You, who are her mother. And because of that, Poison gets upset? For which reason he tries to rape me? It doesn't make sense to me. What does it all mean?"

"He came to me, Fofo. He came here."

"What!!!"

"He came here and turned me into a leper."

"So that was why the woman in the third room didn't respond to Odarley's greeting?"

"Yes. And why you should also go away from here. Because he told me he would find you."

"Me?"

"Yes. And he swore to replace Baby T with you if we made him angry."

"Replace? Make him angry? What are you saying mother? What is all this roundabout talk?"

"Look. Fofo, please, go away."

The sleeping anger in Fofo awakened. "It's all you keep telling me. Go away; go away!" Fofo yelled, "How do I just go away somewhere, mother? Where should I go? I have nothing on me. I got a job at the vegetables market just a few days ago. I tried to stop stealing. But the little I had on me too, I just lost to Macho. So tell me something better."

"I have nothing better to tell you, child. And no money to give you too." Maa Tsuru cried, "I looked on and allowed something to happen that shouldn't have. My hands are tied. I have my finger between his teeth. If I hit him on the head, I'll make him chew off my own finger too inside his mouth. Then what would happen to them?" pointing again at her sons, "Look at them," she went on, no longer crying but clearly hurting, "What have they done? Their only wrong doing is that they came into the world through me."

Rage gripped Fofo. "Is their father still your husband? You said he left, no?"

Maa Tsuru broke down. She began to cry again. "Don't talk to me like that, Fofo," she sniffed, "Just because I made a lot of mistakes in life and I am poor doesn't make me less your mother. So don't talk to me that way."

Fofo's heart churned. She looked at her mother long and then turned her face away. "I don't like coming to see you, mother," she began slowly, "Odarley's mother sacks her like a fowl when she goes to see her. She says Odarley is a thief. You don't sack me when I come to see you. Yet, I don't like coming to see you because I don't like what I feel when I come to see you, mother. I don't."

Maa Tsuru looked away and stared into the outside void

through the tiny window. Fofo's outpouring didn't shock her. It wasn't the first time Fofo had said this to her. But somewhere inside her she said a silent prayer, that somehow something would happen to make it the last.

"Mother," Fofo resumed. Her voice was calm and steady. Too calm and too steady, "why was Poison upset about Maami Broni coming to tell you about Baby T?"

"He didn't want me to know that Baby T was dead."

"Just that?"

Maa Tsuru pursed her lips and refused to respond.

"But Maami Broni came to tell you anyway."

"Yes. She was afraid. If Baby T was made out, someone was bound to remember that she was staying with her."

Fofo felt exhausted. "Did anyone say what happened? Why Baby T died?"

"Poison only said it was Baby T's own fault."

Fofo digested that. And chuckled bitterly. "So how do you feel, mother?"

"How I feel? How am I supposed to feel? How do you suppose I should feel? Do you know what Poison told me to the face? That Baby T ceased to be my daughter the day I sold her to the streets. I sold her to the streets? I sold my own daughter to the streets? Oh God!" she broke down again.

Fofo remained calm and unimpressed.

"I carried her for nine months in my womb." Maa Tsuru cried on. "I screamed in pain when I was bringing her forth. And look where she ended up dying? Under the open skies behind a kiosk at the market place? And all I have left is my anger at the world. Oh God!" And noticed Fofo studying the blue and white plastic rattan bag in the corner near the bed. "Do you need it?" she asked Fofo; calmly, thinking Fofo needed it to pack in her few belongings and get away from Accra.

Fofo turned her attention from the bag, and it was like she had aged ten years more within the last few seconds.

"I can give it to you if you need it." Maa Tsuru offered.

"I don't need the bag," Fofo retorted. "Does he have some things inside?"

"A few of his clothes. Yes. He left without warning. He just left."

"I don't really care about that, mother." Fofo snapped and rose to the bag, thankful for her stepfather's smallish frame. She unzipped it. Inside was sparse. The leftovers of a man neither here nor there. Not there for the wife, not there for the sons, yet, not gone completely from their lives either. She rummaged through and picked out an old pair of shorts; a faded checkered shirt torn at one shoulder; and a crumbled old baseball cap which still carried a pungent smell. Her four-year-old stepbrother was up by the time she was through with her pick and was all over Maa Tsuru on the bed like his baby brother. Fofo paid them no attention.

"I'm off!" she announced brusquely; and stepped out of the room.

"Is everything all right?" Odarley asked anxiously.

"No."

"What was all the long talk about?"

"A lot of bad things. Let's get out of here."

Naa Yomo was still seated on her stool in front of her room. They ignored her. She also did not call them back.

"What bad things?" Odarley asked when they were outside the house.

"I can't talk about it." Fofo sniped.

Odarley frowned. Fofo sometimes acted strange and talked weird. Her sudden decision days ago to go at life alone and detach herself from the gang and to go and scrub carrots and quit drinking were to Odarley, really strange. Who went at life alone at Sodom and Gomorrah?

"Fofo," she called, wanting to make conversation to get Fofo to talk.

"Hm."

"Do you remember what you said the other time? That you knew poverty?"

"Yes. I saw it."

A woman walking close behind them concluded right away that Fofo must be high on something. Drugs after all, flew freely at Sodom and Gomorrah.

"You saw poverty?" Odarley asked, suppressing a chuckle.

"Yes."

"Head to toe?"

"Head to toe. It's face; it's ugly square head; it's big fat toes. I know its shape like . . ."

"You do?"

The woman behind them shook her head sadly.

"Yes," Fofo went on to Odarley, "I know its length and its breadth and its width and its stench."

"You smelt it too?"

"Yes." And poked a forefinger into one nostril.

Odarley winced for her friend. It was all a joke for her but it definitely wasn't for Fofo. It was with a raw passionate rage that she poked the finger inside the nostril.

"What is it?" Odarley persisted.

The woman behind them decided at this point, and to her own peril, not to mind her own business. "Your friend," she addressed Odarley, "why don't you send her to her mother if she is around here!"

Fofo stopped dead in her track so abruptly that the woman landed right into her and lost balance.

"Foolish girl!" the woman yelled, "Have you seen what you nearly did? Were you dreaming or what? Or is it some of those your stupid drugs and the *devil's leaf* working you up?"

Fofo was by now in high dudgeon. One look upon her face when she swung round, and the woman realized too late that she should have minded her own business.

"Yes, I am dreaming!" Fofo spat with a calmness that was

menacing and akin to a simmering volcano, "I had a very bad dream last night. That is normality with me. But today, having set eyes on your 50-80-50 shape, I am sure to have the nightmare of a good dream."

The woman gasped. "How dare you!" she wailed, "My youngest grand daughter is even older than you! How dare you!"

"And how dare you also poke your nose into my matter and call me foolish girl?" Fofo retorted, "Do you also know how old the youngest of my daughters is? Guess it for yourself. That is her!" and pointed at a befuddled Odarley, "Take your guess. And now tell me. When you were my age, did you have a daughter her age?"

The woman began to sweat profusely. "I don't blame you!" she wheezed, "After all, we are just a stone throw from Sodom and Gomorrah. Were we to be somewhere else where being an adult counted, you would have seen what I would have done to you." And thudded off.

Odarley burst out laughing. Fofo joined in. Then suddenly she stopped and said," Odarley, we part ways here."

Odarley's laughter froze. "Why?"

"No whys. Go your way. I'll see you this evening."

"Why?" Odarley was sad and astounded.

"I said, no whys. Go."

"Will you come to us in the night?"

"I don't know."

"And Poison?"

"I'll see you, Odarley. Go!" And took off in the opposite direction, not looking back even once.

4

Kabria's household was up to the chin in their routine Monday morning chaos. She was up with the crow and still running around. Obea, when she woke up, came first into the living room to switch on the radio. She put the dial on Harvest FM, went back into the room to make her bed, swept the veranda, brushed her teeth, and for whatever odd reason, chose to keep the toothbrush in her mouth throughout laying the breakfast table.

Kabria decided to let that remain Obea's problem. If she wanted to have her toothbrush for breakfast, fine.

Adade was in the bedroom listening to something on another FM station on the bedside radio. And Abena, the househelp, was tidying up the kitchen. She had to hurry up to go to her apprentice dressmaking job. Kabria prepared Essie and Ottu's lunchboxes. Harvest FM was reviewing the morning newspapers. Kofi Annan's name kept cropping up. Kabria wondered how many people in other parts of the world had heard of Ghana before Annan's appointment as the first black African to head the United Nations.

Ottu, who should have been up and brushing his teeth, was still in his room, which was adjoined to Kabria's and Adade's.

"Ottu!" Kabria called.

No response. But Kabria could bet her teeth that Ottu had heard her all right.

Essie was polishing shoes on the porch. Kabria called her. But

Kabria calling her right after calling Ottu, who did not respond, made Essie suspect what was coming. That she was going to be sent to go and call Ottu. And Essie did not want to perform a task like that on a Monday morning, knowing what would ensue. At best a squabble. Many times, a battle of nerves. So why go call Ottu in the room when she could just as effectively deal with the matter without moving an inch? She took matters into her own hands, grumbled, inhaled air like an albatross, and howled, "Ottuuuu . . .!" at a pitch that could have woken up the dead in the Arctic.

It was Adade who reacted to the madness. And in the typical Ghanaian fathers fashion where the 'culprit's' mother is queried instead of the 'culprit'.

"Kabria," he poked his head through the bedroom door, "can you tell your daughter that the sun is still not fully up? Why do you let her scream like that?" And retreated into the room.

Ottu emerged from his room shortly after. The frown on his face said it all. That he was ordered out by his father. Man to man showdown.

Kabria tried to play the peacemaker. "Essie, did you have to do that?"

But Ottu had no appreciation for her efforts. He eyed her and deepened his frown. Essie however, was not going to sit quiet and accept a blame she wasn't convinced was hers.

"Mum," she moaned, "Ottu has a blockage in his ears. Haven't you noticed?"

The presenter on Harvest FM, Sylv Po, saved the situation. His strong voice announced a coming discussion on HIV AIDS to be featured on his 'Good Morning Ghana' show. Kabria proceeded to pack Ottu's snack. Then it occurred to her that Obea was still in the bathroom. And unless she was delivering twins, she should have been out of there long ago.

"Obea!" she called.

Obea responded graciously.

"Are you still in the bathroom?"

"Yes, Mum."

"Why? What are you still doing in there?"

"I am washing soap off my body, Mum."

Adade emerged from the bedroom just then, buttoning a cuff. "Why is it you and your children always turn this house into a concert hall every morning?"

"My children?" Kabria thumbed her chest.

Adade ignored her and sat down to breakfast.

Kabria went into the kitchen to fry his eggs. By the time she rejoined him at the table, Adade's head was buried in a newspaper.

"Adade," Kabria sought to gain his attention.

"Hm." Still immersed in the paper.

"Creamy is giving me headaches again. The mechanic said . . ."

"Kabria!" his head shot up from over the newspaper, "Can we talk about this after work?"

Sylv Po's female studio guest was on and complaining about the AIDS prevention campaign not driving home the message of abstinence and faithfulness with the same intensity as the use of condoms. Then she touched on the AIDS issue versus the street-children phenomenon.

"You see," she went on, "there is a lot of pain and hopelessness out there on the streets which many seek to deal with through drugs, sex, and alchohol. During a recent survey we conducted for a programme, all the girls we talked to out there were already very sexually active. And we also established that, for many of them, rape was their first sexual experience. And I am talking about girls as young as seven. Many were child prostitutes. They had no idea at all about the extent of self-damage to themselves. Sex to them was just a convenient means of survival. Many were roaming about, oblivious to whether or not they were HIV positive, so . . ."

"Mum," Essie barged into Kabria's concentration, "Do you know that Obea is still in the room?"

Kabria was hurtled back into her world and to the welcoming sight of Ottu who was standing beside one armchair and holding one sock in one hand.

"Why are you standing there with one sock?" Kabria asked him.

"I don't know." He replied coolly with a shrug.

Adade who was finishing his breakfast was still engrossed in his papers.

"You don't know why you are standing there and holding one sock?"

Ottu sensed the growing irritation in Kabria's tone. "I know," he replied; but continued to stand there anyway, with the one sock; not in the least perturbed by Kabria's crossness.

Kabria dipped quickly into her reserves to top up her patience and succeeded in asking with the calmness of a saint. "Since you know, would you mind telling me?"

"What?"

Kabria sighed in exasperation. "Why you are holding one sock?"

"Because I can't find the other."

Kabria had to top up her patience very quickly again. Then she asked, "Where did you find this one?"

"Inside my shoe." Ottu Mumbled.

"And was the other sock not inside the other shoe?"

"I didn't find the other shoe. Have you seen it?"

Kabria's patience became depleted. "No, I haven't!" in a tone that spoke volumes, "Do I wear it with you?"

Ottu uttered not one word again. He went down on his knees, searched, and found the other shoe under the armchair.

Kabria's mind reverted to Obea. "What are you still doing in the room?" she reproached.

Obea didn't respond.

Kabria headed straight to the girls' room in a blaze and swung their door open without the courtesy of a knock. And caught Obea just in time, hastily push something under her pillow. Kabria didn't react. Her instincts told her not to. And she never resisted her instincts.

"Are you coming?" she calmly asked Obea who was all dressed up and ready.

"Yes." Obea replied flatly. She did not look Kabria in the face.

Adade announced from the living room that he was off. Kabria bid him goodbye but remained where she stood. Obea realized in good time that Kabria had no intention of leaving without her. She rose. Kabria made way for her to pass; sized the bulging pillow and left for her own room. Their bedside radio was still on. She shifted the dial to Harvest FM. Sylv Po's studio guest was saying, "Some individuals and religious bodies still frown upon sex education. They argue that it encourages promiscuity. But research has proven otherwise. So parents and guardians must be involved. And even if their children do not always follow their advice, they still remain, potentially, the children's most influential sources of information. Their active involvement will reinforce messages at the interpersonal level at home."

Kabria's mind wandered onto the hidden mystery under Obea's pillow. She dressed on in silence, turned off the radio and told the children to get their bags into the car. She picked her bag, took the car key, had a final look at herself in the mirror and satisfied with her reflection, left the room.

"Go on ahead into the car," she told them.

Essie was the first. Ottu followed. Obea hesitated briefly and then joined them. Kabria turned towards the girls' room. This time, her instincts didn't hold her back. She got to Obea's bed and lifted the pillow. It was an old exercise book. 'Why was Obea hiding an exercise book from her?' She picked it up. Some pamphlets fell out. The title Planned Parenthood Association of Ghana hit her in the face like hot steam. She turned the first one over. *Sexual Health For Quality Life?* Her heart raced. Sexual health? Was Obea into or about to . . . Oh God! Please God! Let it not be! Please!

"Mum, we are sweating. We'll be late!" Ottu yelled from outside.

Kabria quickly replaced the exercise book and its contents as she found them and dashed back to the living room. Abena was outside, opening the gate. Her workplace was ten minutes walk away.

"What were you doing inside?" Ottu asked.

"A couple of things." Kabria replied.

Creamy behaved like the civilized self propelled four wheeled vehicle Kabria loved to believe it was - until she reached the children's school. And then it refused to budge.

Kabria humped one desperate foot down onto the accelerator. The force of her fury infuriated Creamy all the more. It squealed like a mouse in a strangler's grip. Kabria's eyes moistened with humiliation. 'Did you have to go off like this right in front of their school gate?' she yelled inside her head.

The children were all out of the car. Ottu quickly disappeared into the schoolyard after thanking God very loudly, to ensure Kabria heard, for his mercy in getting him safely to school before 'this disgrace'.

Essie was almost at the gate when she heard the first squeal of Creamy. She halted to attention. Then turned and smiled. And froze the smile as though an Arctic breeze had blown past her lips. Two mates of hers at that very instant, alighted simultaneously from their respective cars. The cars' fine engines zoomed soundlessly off right after. Essie's left corner smile defrosted at the sight of it while the right lip corner remained frozen.

Obea approached Creamy. "Mum," she cried, "this is the greatest and most embarrassing moment of my life!"

Kabria felt tempted to bring up the discovery under her pillow to shut her up. Instead, she said, "Go on in."

Essie, who followed Obea to the car, wailed, "Mum. Why can't you just buy a new car?"

"They will laugh at us!" Obea added.

Kabria grew irritated. She had, what to her were some real problems, to deal with. She had to, for instance, get to the office in time in order to later pick up her garden eggs and tomatoes from her regular vendors at the Agbogbloshie market, preferably before noon. Those were real and practical problems to moan about. "Those you are afraid will laugh at you because your Mum's car developed a hitch," she began, "what do they do to those pupils who come by *tro-tro* and on foot?"

No one replied. They swung round and walked away.

Kabria was smiling off her frustration when she heard someone call, "Madam."

It was a taxi driver who came to drop some school children. "Wait small and spark again," he advised.

Kabria hesitated, but had no choice but to agree. Ten minutes later, Creamy was back in motion.

Two weeks ago her mechanic had recommended some repair work. She had been suspicious because of the enthusiasm with which the mechanic made the suggestion. He had sounded too eager, and caused her to conclude that he was just out to strike gold in the mines of her poor Creamy. Now she couldn't help wondering if maybe she had been unreasonable in that suspicion.

"Peeeeee . . ." a driver behind her in a red Mazda honked into her thoughts. She ignored him. It was obvious he wanted her to drive faster. It was a wish she definitely could not grant him. The rate at which she was going was the fastest Creamy could go. The driver of a yellow and white Opel Kadett taxi who was somewhere behind the red Mazda, obviously did not possess the kind of patience that was content to stop at just honking. He ventured out of the lane and swore when he narrowly missed crashing into an oncoming black Hyundai. He tooted his horn when he levelled with Kabria, and upon gaining her attention, parcelled his anger at her in a ton of obscenities. Kabria ignored him. No way was she going to utter such unprintable insults back at him. But her aloofness only infuriated the taxi driver more. "Foolish woman," he roared, "clear that piece of outdated metal rubbish off the road!" and zoomed off.

That got Kabria pondering over whether maybe it wasn't high time Adade started dropping the children at school. That, though, would mean the children getting up earlier and hurrying with their chores, which could translate into more grumbling; more chaos, more excitement! No. There had to be another way. Maybe she could find a new job that paid better. But the thought of it filled her with horror. A new job could mean a better pay cheque; but it could come with monotony and a stringent work schedule. Her job at MUTE was flexible and enabled her to be there enough for the children. And the office's relaxed and informal atmosphere suited her fine. She couldn't eat her cake and have it.

The traffic lights ahead turned amber. Two indisciplined drivers sped recklessly past her to beat the red. Kabria didn't need to slow to a halt. The light was red long before she got to it. A girl of about eight, holding the hand of a blind woman walked up to her. The woman launched into an obviously well rehearsed chorus line, invoking God's blessings upon Kabria if she parted with something.

"Is that your child?" Kabria asked her.

"Yes," the woman replied with zeal.

"Shouldn't she be in school?" Kabria asked.

The woman sensed that no money would be forthcoming, only questions. She became irritated. "If people like you won't give me money, how can I send her to school?" she snapped, "I beg you. If you won't give me anything, don't come and preach to me too on top. Keep your money and go away with that your bad luck blazing red lips." And yelled at the girl, "Move!"

Blazing red lips? Had a miracle just occurred? She did have on a blazing red lipstick!

"Pi . . ." a horn tooted.

Kabria looked at the traffic light. She thought it must have turned green too soon. It hadn't. The car behind her was calling her attention.

"Pi . . ." again. It sounded so soft and so smooth it was like pure silk. Yes. Even in the world of car horns, there were grades and classes too. She turned to its source. And there it was. At par with Creamy. Navy blue. Gleaming like polished marble. The hum of its engine, music to the ears, making nonsense of Creamy in all aspects. Where from this sleek masterpiece? And where in the four corners of Ghana was the cash that afforded people such luxuries, hidden?

The sleek windowpane slid smoothly down. "Kabria," the female voice behind the steering wheel called, "is that really you?"

Kabria took a good look and recognized her. She found herself grappling for words. What she wanted to say, failed to find voice. She felt Ms. Sleek scrutinize Creamy. Or was it her imagination? The green light came on. "Oooops!" Ms Sleek exclaimed, "See you!" And glided off like a sailing bird. By the time the car's sleeky tail end disappeared, Kabria was still applying feet to Creamy's clutch and accelerator. A classic case of one of fate's dubious ping-pong games. Ms Sleek was the all and all Miss-Always-Last-In-Class at secondary school. She didn't progress beyond there. Her talent obviously lay somewhere else, outside academe. Ms. Sleek occupied Kabria the next few minutes and caused the outbreak of a protest hormone reaction, which engulfed her from head to toe. Her permed hair was limp with sweat and misery by the time she arrived at the office.

MUTE, where Kabria worked, was a non-governmental organization founded by its boss, Dina. And MUTE was just that: Mute. As in silence. Not an acronym.

Dina was a graduate of the University of Ghana. Her marriage to her campus boyfriend shortly after her graduation, ended in divorce after four turbulent years of childlessness. Finding herself with no child and no husband and plenty of time, she recollected her frustration during her final year research work for her major essay when she found out that regular libraries did not stock the kind of information she was looking for. And with that recollection, came the birth of the idea for MUTE.

Kabria's job entailed sometimes going out into the field to research and talk to people for information and verification. But mostly, she sat behind her working table to sift and sort out and write reports for their documentation centre which Dina fondly referred to as: The Alternative Library. Every social, gender and child issue was of interest to MUTE. Their sources were newspapers, magazines, radio, television, hearsay, gossip, telephone calls, and observations. On a few occasions, Kabria or another of her co-workers had had to play the investigative reporter.

Dina breezed out of her office with a frown on hearing Kabria's voice.

"Dina. Hello. Good morning!" Kabria greeted her boss cheerfully.

Dina did not respond. She took a long sullen look at her wristwatch and then at Kabria. The message hit Kabria loud and clear. She jumped to her own defense.

"It was Creamy, Dina. It went off right in front of the children's school. Can you believe that?"

Dina's frown cleared. "If Creamy could talk, it would always be fighting you!" she hurled back, "You push everything down its throat."

"That is because of the many problems it also coughs up for me in spite of my loyalty and absolute faithfulness to it."

Vickie, a co-worker, chuckled, "Kabria, we all know you too well. Even if you go and knock down some groundnut seller's ware at Makola Square, you would find a way to put the blame on Creamy."

They all began to laugh. Then Dina cut in and said, "I have a couple of meetings to attend this morning. We might be getting some support for the project on mentally ill pregnant women. One of the TV stations is even warming up to the idea of a documentary film if we come up with a good report."

"Thank God!" Kabria exclaimed.

"If only we could get hold of one such perverse men who sleep with them." Aggie, the last of the foursome, lamented.

"I think we should use the mentally ill pregnant woman near the lagoon vulcaniser as our case study." Kabria suggested.

"I think so too." Vickie agreed, "The vulcaniser seemed to know a lot. He said many of the area's wee smokers take turns with her when they are *high*."

"That definitely is worth considering." Dina observed. And turned towards her office.

"Oh, Dina," Aggie called, "that aluminium factory manager, will you be seeing him too?"

"Yes. Why?"

Aggie winked and giggled, "I hear he is *veeeery* good looking."

Dina glared back playfully and retorted, "And *veeeery* married. Didn't you hear that one too?"

They all laughed again. "And Aggie," Dina went on, "Vickie is the only one among us here who is yet to taste marriage. Think more of her in your match-making fantasies, will you?"

"Me?" Vickie howled, "Me who is sworn to celibacy?"

"Of course," Kabria shrieked, "just as I too am also an Eskimo princess." And while the others still laughed added, "Can you believe that a blind woman begging by the roadside just insulted me to go away with my blazing red lips?"

"She saw your lipstick?" Vickie yelled.

"Instant healing, I tell you!" Kabria quipped.

The office shook with more laughter.

Dina emerged shortly from her office en route to her meetings. "Will you go to the Agbogbloshie market today? I need some things." She asked Kabria.

"Oh boss," Kabria teased, "considering the time I reported for work today, even if I wasn't intending to go, I would have to, just for you. Wouldn't I?"

"Don't sweet talk me!" Dina laughed, "Do I look that much

like Adade for you to mistake me for him?" and amidst more laughter, gave her market list and some money to Kabria.

5

Creamy sent Kabria safe and sound to the market. No hitch. And Agbogbloshie's human and vehicular traffic was heavy as usual. She sought a slope to park, knowing how unpredictable Creamy sometimes could be. One moment well behaved, the next moment bonkers. Uphill, she could always put the gear in free and roll down, if Creamy failed to start.

Where she parked was quite a distance from the market. She headed first to the garden eggs vendor, stopping briefly on the way to get some fresh red and green peppers for Dina. The garden eggs woman broke into a bright smile under her broad straw hat at the sight of Kabria. And rose. Her large frame was completely submerged in a huge flowered light blue *fos* dress, which Kabria concluded at first glance to be not less than three times her size. The woman once explained that it afforded her some much needed freedom and plenty of fresh air. She threw another smile in Kabria's direction and dragged a big basketful of garden eggs from under a table nearby. Special selection for her regular customers.

"The usual?" she beamed at Kabria.

"Yes. And my boss also wants half a basket."

The woman's smile widened. More sales; a good day. She adjusted the measuring basket on the low broad table on which she retailed the garden eggs; filled it with some of the selected ones, expertly overturned it into a black plastic bag, and repeated the process with Dina's too.

"Did you come with your car?" she asked Kabria as she tied it up.

"Yes."

"Where did you park?"

Kabria told her.

"All the way up there?"

Kabria was not going to lay bare Creamy's misdemeanors. "Yes. I wanted to do a little exercise." She paid and collected the ware and decided she would unload the garden eggs in Creamy and then hire a *kayayoo* when she bought the tomatoes, which in addition to Dina's, would be a lot.

"Did any of the tomato lorries come today?" she asked the garden eggs woman.

"Oh, if you are buying a lot, then I'll advise against today. Only two lorries from the Upper Region came. Very expensive."

"Hard luck for me then. Thanks anyway." And turned to leave.

"I'll advise again that you don't take the short route, Madam," the woman shot back, "A girl died there last week. A very gruesome and peculiar death. People still throng there."

Kabria remembered. "Yes. I think I heard of it. Was she a kayayoo?" — porters from the North who come to South

"That was what some people said. But others also alleged she was of the streets."

"A street girl?"

"No. Street worker. You know . . ."

"Oh, I see."

"Very sad, I tell you. I saw her. Unbelievable. Her face was so mutilated . . . and her head . . . ah! That too was completely shaven." And shook her head slowly. "In fact, all the hair on every part of her body. Ah, Madam, I tell you, whoever did that to her could not have had a soul. The person definitely has no soul. Then the following day, fresh blood and some white feathers were found there. A white fowl was apparently slaughtered there secretly the night after. If you ask me, it was to appease the girl's soul. Anyway, so as I said, don't pass there."

"I won't." And thanked her. She went and disposed of the garden eggs, and took the long route to the tomatoes vendor, who confirmed the scarcity of tomatoes and added, "I didn't leave plenty for you, Madam. It was too expensive. And if it weren't because I was expecting my regular Monday customers like yourself, I would probably not even have bought any at all from the wholesalers. So if you like, buy just a little and come back on Wednesday."

Kabria complied. And set off with the little in a plastic bag towards the same long route by which she came. But where just minutes ago, there had been a free flow of human traffic, a sea of spectators had now invaded a spot along it and were enjoying a gratis boxing spree between two very muscular heavy duty porters who were settling a disagreement over their operational boundaries and areas of control through the power of their fists. Kabria stopped a distance away from the unorthodox boxing ring. A woman who had apparently decided to make a roundabout turn, spat angrily as she scrambled past Kabria, "Big muscles, tiny brains. Can we normal ones ever understand these street people?"

'Normal people? Street people?' Kabria wondered. She couldn't wait to get to the office to tell it. Was that the perception? Were people living on the streets deemed not normal? She too made a roundabout turn to go via the short route just when some of the 'boxing' spectators began shouting for the police because the muscled men had both pulled out knives. When she reached the tragic scene of the previous week, she saw a handful of people there satisfying their curiosity.

"My sister," one of two women beside whom Kabria also paused to take in the scene, began, "The way they say they did her face and other things, I tell you, her ghost will not rest. It will hover among the living until the right thing is done."

But her friend was obviously a doubting Thomas. "Ho! What right thing?" she sniped, "Didn't they say someone slaughtered a white fowl here the night after? If I were she, I would accept my one white fowl like that and go in peace to my spirit world. Ah! If the ghosts of all the people who die here at Agbogbloshie and whose bodies are never claimed and who end up buried in mass graves at Mile Eleven should decide to hover around here amongst us, wouldn't we be bumping into more ghosts than human beings during market days?"

Kabria could neither laugh nor cry. She took some steps closer to the spot. Her handbag was slung on her left shoulder with the plastic bag of fresh tomatoes in her right hand. And the nearer she got there, the more her curiosity got the better of her.

"They say she wasn't killed here, oh!" someone proffered.

"That was what I also heard!" another responded.

"Oh, life!" lamented a third, "To think that she was carried inside somebody's womb for a whole nine months. Only to end up here? She was also completely naked, they said."

"Eeeeh?"

"Yes."

"Was she sent to Korle-Bu for an autopsy?" Kabria found herself driven to inquire.

"I think so," the first woman replied, "by all means the police and the Metropolitan Assembly people will send her there. It's a coroner's case so they'll do a post mortem and then send the body to the mortuary. If the body is not claimed after a while, then straight to Mile Eleven."

"Oh Jeez!" the second woman muttered, "What rest and everlasting peace can such a soul find? I hear they are put in wawa coffins and packed like sardines into refuse trucks. What . . ."

"Agoo . . . agoo . . ." a voice shouted from behind Kabria.

Kabria shifted to make way. Then obeying her instincts, turned swiftly. Her eyes fell directly upon the face of a boy, fourteen or fifteen thereabouts. She became jittery. There was something peculiar about him. And about the way he gawked at her from under the old and crumpled baseball cap he wore. Their eyes locked for a second. Then he turned and resumed shouting, "Agoo–agoo–"

with renewed urgency. He was too much in a haste to vamoose from the scene. Suddenly, a woman screamed, "Get him! Don't let him go! He's got somebody's purse."

Anxious hands plunged into pockets and bags. The scene lost its original focus of attention. The boy was hotly pursued. Kabria looked up from frisking through her bag. All eyes were on her. Everyone else had stopped searching for their purses in their bags. She was the only one still searching. She felt her knees go weak. A flurry of excitement gripped the teeming crowd. "They have him!" someone yelled, "He's been caught!"

They dragged him back. Kabria remained rooted in awe. She was handed back her purse. The increasing crowd grew eager to make history of the boy. A hand materialized from nowhere and whacked him across the face. The boy wailed shrilly. Kabria's stomach churned. A man started looking around for a stick. "I'll whip him till he sees his guardian angel!" the man threatened. The crowd thickened. Excitement mounted. But in the midst of it a ray of reasoning hit Kabria. If anything happened to the boy, it would be on her conscience. Time was flying. He could have been her son. He looked to be about Obea's age. He should have been in the classroom learning. He should have been sending his mother's pulse racing with an exercise book containing PPAG pamphlets under his pillow and complaining about his mother embarrassing him with her old car and not be out here pick pocketing. His survival should have been some adult's responsibility. "Tettey! Tettey! Is that not you?" Kabria screamed through the commotion, "Oh God! Tettey! It's you! Don't you remember me? It's me. Auntie Tsoo. Have you forgotten me? Eh?"

By which time she had meandered her way close to the boy who looked like he was praying for the earth to open and swallow him up. He tried to say something, stuttered badly, and made no sense.

"Leave him alone, please!" Kabria cried, "Please, leave him to me. I know him. I know him."

The boy began to sob. A man holding him by one arm jostled

him to and fro. "You want us to let a thief go free?" he glared at Kabria."

"No." Kabria cried, "Hand him over to me. Please."

The man sized her up and down. He wasn't at all pleased. The crowd looked on expectantly. Kabria's instincts took charge. She opened her purse and took out some notes. She offered them to the man. "Please," she begged, "let go of him."

The man stared at the notes, snatched them from Kabria, snorted at the boy, "Lucky you!" and let go of the boy's arm. And when no one expected it, knocked the boy's forehead with his knuckle. The boy sobbed some more.

"Thank you! Thank you very much!" Kabria whimpered. She was shaking like a leaf. She grabbed the boy's hand and hastened away from the crowd with him. She felt the bewildered stares following them like the weight of a ton around her neck. "Hurry up before someone changes his or her mind!" she hissed at the boy.

A woman they passed selling crabs yelled, "These thieves; I don't know if they are born bad or made bad. No matter what you do to them, once they have sworn to steal, it's that they'll do. Wash and starch them, dry them, iron them, and they will still steal. Chia!"

They were still in hostile territory. "Hurry up!" Kabria ordered him. Then he did something spontaneous. He took Kabria's bag of tomatoes in one hand and placed his free hand in Kabria's. She looked down at him in surprise. He smiled up at her. They walked on in silence to Creamy. She took the tomatoes from him and said; "Now you are safe. Go!"

She expected him to thank her and turn round and dash off. Instead, he remained exactly where he was.

"Did you understand what I said?" Kabria asked him.

He nodded.

"So what are you waiting for?"

He didn't respond.

"What is it?"

He didn't reply.

Kabria wondered. "Have you eaten? Are you hungry?"

He nodded.

Kabria chuckled. "I don't suppose you are expecting me to give you money for food, are you?"

He bowed his head and drew with his toe in the ground.

Kabria grew exasperated. "You tried to steal my purse. I saved you at a cost. And now I should feed you too?"

The boy continued to draw in the ground. Kabria gruntled and took out a note from her purse for him. He took it, stared at it, Mumbled a thank you and remained.

"What again?" Kabria snapped.

He didn't speak.

Kabria looked at her time. "Look," she said sharply, "I must go now."

He nodded.

Kabria grew desperate. She opened her purse and took out another thousand note and handed it over to him. He snatched it. Kabria became irritated. "A very expensive thief it is you have turned out to be, young man. I, your intended victim who bailed you out, has to feed you too?" and got into Creamy. She started it. Creamy didn't respond. Kabria looked into the driving mirror. The boy was still standing there. He pushed back the cap. Kabria gasped and turned off the ignition. She took another good look of him. Then she got out of the car, because ruggedness, dirt and all, the good-looking face she was staring into was not handsome. It was pretty.

"Hey!" Kabria exclaimed.

Pretty face smiled shyly. "I am a girl," she said.

Kabria wanted to laugh and cry and do the *mapuka* all in one. "A girl who posed as a boy to steal my purse? Do you have a name?"

"Yes. Fofo."

"Fofo?" and Kabria pinched herself. The pain she felt told her that everything was real and actually happening. "Look," she managed at last, "this is all a bit weird and unexpected and just too much. I am not sure of what to do with you or what you want me to . . ."

"Government!" the girl cut in.

Kabria cocked her eyebrows. She wasn't sure she heard right, because it didn't make sense. "What did you say?"

"I said government. I want government."

Kabria roared into laughter. She laughed till she shed some tears and then laughed some more. "You want the government?"

Fofo didn't reply. She wore a hurt look.

Two words hit Kabria. Crazy! Vamoose! "Look," she said, "I have my work and other responsibilities to return to. Do you live around here?"

Fofo nodded.

"Good. Listen. Maybe I'll come back here tomorrow. If I do, I will park my car at this same spot. If you want to, you can meet me here before noon. Is that all right with you?"

Fofo nodded again.

Kabria felt a pang of guilt. She didn't mean what she said. Indeed, unless the unexpected should happen, she had no intention at all of returning to Agbogbloshie the following day. She had said what she did only to create an escape avenue. Fofo however gained some glimmer of hope with the proposition. It cleared away her look of pain. Kabria noticed it but suppressed her guilt and got into Creamy. "God should be able to forgive me this little lie, or?" she sought to comfort herself. And turned on the ignition. Creamy whined. She humped down a foot on the clutch and shifted the gear into free. Fofo's face clouded again. Kabria wondered if Fofo had seen through her lie. She released the handbrake. Creamy began to roll down the slope. Fofo got into stride alongside it. Kabria coaxed the accelerator and started it. Creamy began to stutter to life. Fofo quickened her pace and hurtled some words into the air.

"What did you say?" Kabria yelled.

"I said, the girl who was found dead last week at where I tried to rob you, was my sister."

Kabria had never felt so grateful to God as she felt at that moment. She was already in the car and rolling further away from Fofo. "Bizzare," she thought, "Fofo was a scatterbrain." And pressed the accelerator further down. Creamy sputtered and coughed and rolled on down. Kabria looked into the mirror. Fofo was standing and staring at the back of Creamy. She was waving. And crying.

At the office when Kabria began spewing out in torrents her ordeal at the market, no one interrupted even once. At the end of it Vickie exclaimed, "Wow!" Aggie sighed heavily. Dina wondered aloud where all this could be leading. And the sight of Fofo waving and crying came back to haunt Kabria. "Just this morning I listened to Sylv Po on Harvest FM touch on the issue of the HIV AIDS pandemic versus the street child. And see what I ran into. And according to gossip at the market, the girl Fofo is claiming to be her sister, was a prostitute."

Dina's creative mind was already in motion. "There could be something to be unravelled in there, you know." She muttered thoughtfully. "A girl at the market who tried to rob someone while dressed as a boy, who wants to meet the government, and who claims a dead suspected prostitute found at the market place was her sister? And you say Harvest FM did a programme this morning on AIDS and streetchildren?"

"Yes."

"Shouldn't we talk to them?"

"On what?" Aggie asked.

"I am not yet exactly sure on what. But I can feel something in there. And if we should do our bit and get more on the girl, we could convince them to do a programme on her. It could be good for us too."

Kabria was all but enthused. "Could this be leading to something like me keeping my promise and going back there tomorrow?"

"Let me talk to Harvest FM first," Dina proffered and went into her office to make the call.

"Do you think they'll fall for it?" Aggie asked the others.

Vickie considered briefly and said, "Who knows? It is a real case of the street children phenomenon. Some gnawing questions could be answered. Like why is she on the streets? There is a story behind every street child out there."

Moreover, how many boy thieves out there are actually girl thieves?" Kabria asked, "That should make an interesting find."

"What about the notion too, that many of the girls on the streets of Accra are northerners who came to seek greener pastures, through working as kayayoos?" Vickie asked, "Fofo doesn't sound northern to me!"

"She isn't." Kabria replied, "She is a Ga."

"In fact, many of them are southerners," Aggie came in, "It is at Sodom and Gomorrah that you find a concentration of many of these young girls from the north, but even there, you have your fair share of southerners. Girls and boys who are not necessarily orphans and who have one or both parents living right here in Accra."

"Why?" Vickie howled, "Why should somebody living right here in Accra and under a secure roof, let go of his or her child on to the streets?"

Dina, who overheard the question as she emerged from her office into the general one shared by the three, retorted, "That is a question Fofo's story may be able to answer. Girls! You won't believe what I just found out from Harvest FM. According to the producer of Sylv Po's 'Good Morning Ghana' show, either Fofo lied to Kabria, or something doesn't quite fit. Apparently, it was Sylv Po who drew the attention of the police that day to the girl's body. It was breaking news on his GMG show, following a call by someone to the studio. Did any of you hear of it that day?"

All three shook their heads.

"Well," Dina went on, "the FM stations are always being bombarded with such calls, aren't they? But now listen to this. Three days later, which means last Thursday, someone called Harvest FM again, to, as she put it, volunteer information about the dead girl. Fofo's purported sister. And according to the caller, the dead girl's name was Fati, who hailed from the north."

"Fati?" all three howled.

"Yes. And that her death was a punishment for something she had done. That she died because she deserted her husband. He was an old man, a friend of her father who had her betrothed to him just a few days after she was born, and who in accordance with tradition, took care of her from infancy, bearing every cost of her upbringing; until she reached puberty, whereupon after her first menstruation, he performed the final marriage rite and took her on, formally, as his wife."

"Fati?" Kabria still could not make sense of it.

"That was what they said the caller alleged." Dina maintained.

"Well," Kabria shook her head, "I was the one who saw and talked with Fofo. And I am more than certain that she is a Ga through and through." "Or maybe she and the dead sister had different fathers. Maybe hers was a Ga man and her sister's was from the north." Vickie contemplated.

"But couldn't she have been lying too?" Aggie wondered about Fofo, "What wouldn't a thief do to gain pity and sympathy. She succeeded in getting you to part with money for her, Kabria. No?" Kabria came to Fofo's defense. "I had given her the money already before she made the claim."

"Then there is only one way left to get to the bottom of it all, isn't it?" Dina implied.

All eyes reverted to Kabria. "I guess so." She conceded.

"Shouldn't we bring in the police?" Vickie wondered.

"Harvest FM has relayed the information to them already. As to whether they will do anything with it, remains another question." Dina divulged, "Though if you ask me, I cannot for the good of me anticipate that the police, with their voluminous backlog of cases and meager resources, would dispatch someone to go and investigate whether a girl found dead in the open at the Agbogbloshie market was indeed a young girl fleeing an unsuitable marriage or the sister of a pickpocket. Does the word: priority, sound familiar to anyone here?"

6

The exercise book with its PPAG pamphlets replaced Fofo and everything to do with her in Kabria's mind when she set off after work to go and pick the children from school. She knew she was going to have to ask Obea some uncomfortable questions. Not only that. She also needed to brace herself for, maybe, some uncomfortable answers too. So alone inside Creamy and in the secrecy of her head, she began to practice how she would approach it.

'Obea, I am your mother, so don't feel shy about . . .' No! Too flat.

'Obea, I know you have reached the age where you and me should have been talking very often about...' No! Too long. Too roundabout. Why go in circles when she could hit the nail right on the head.

'Obea, tell me. What do you make of all the talk about AIDS and STDs and teenage pregnancy? Don't you think it can start with . . .'

'Jeez! Kabria! That is pathetic!' she chided herself, 'No! No! No! No! No! Why jump to conclusions and think the worst of your daughter?'

Okay, another try: 'Obea, when I came to call you this morning, I noticed you push something under your pillow. Later, I snooped and found an exercise book with PPAG pamphlets. Would you want us to talk about it?'

Not bad. But what if instead of the expected "Yes" reply to

the last question, Obea said a polite, "No"? One could never be sure of Obea's generation. They were a different ball game altogether. When she was Obea's age, she used to wait to be asked questions by her parents before she answered. And when she did, it was with her hands behind her and her head bowed as a show of respect. Her children, nowadays, sometimes looked her straight in the face and bawled out replies to questions she was still formulating in her head. They say to her with the ease of a downward flow, things that took her all the bravery she could summon to even just fantasize about saying to her mother. Her own mother never talked about boyfriends with her, let alone sex. She lived, it seemed, under the assumption that Kabria would never talk to a man till the day she was destined to marry; when the Holy Ghost would somehow conjure the most befitting groom by her side to exchange her 'I do' with. And although Kabria would be doing and saying and learning everything for the first time, she would get it all right and crisply perfect. Well, those were the days. Now, her children were living with a threat called AIDS. So, what her mother in her time could afford not to do with her as a growing daughter, she had no option but to do it with her growing daughter.

She spotted Obea right away when she reached the school gate. She was sitting under a tree with some classmates and they were locked in what appeared to her to be an intense tete-a-tete. Her rehearsals in the car threatened to dissipate into thin air. What were they discussing? Were they comparing notes about boyfriends perhaps? She quickly checked herself. 'This is not your generation, Kabria,' she reminded herself, 'This is Obea's generation. Communicate with her. Do not upset yourself with suspicions. Find out the facts.' She inhaled deeply and looked around. Essie, who was playing with a friend nearby, didn't look too excited at the sight of Kabria. Evidently she would have loved to play some more. Ottu was nowhere around. Kabria prayed that he spotted her soon and came over. But he was still nowhere in sight by the time Obea and Essie picked their bags and came to the car. Kabria asked Essie to wait by Creamy and went with Obea to look for him. Obea went to his classroom to check while Kabria waited by the school gate. Obea returned with him shortly after, and the look on his face prompted Kabria to ask him which of them ought to be wearing a frown. "Why weren't you outside?" she asked him.

"You were late!" he retorted.

"That is no answer to the question!" Kabria protested.

Ottu frowned some more and growled, "Because you were late, Essie said I was a naughty boy."

Kabria scowled. Where is the connection? "What has my being late got to do with you and Essie fracassing?" she asked.

Ottu pointed at Essie and howled, "She said I was naughty!"

"Yes," Essie grizzled, "Because you . . ."

"Stop it!" Kabria intervened, "Get into the car. Both of you!" And instantly, her problems with Creamy; the drama with Fofo; and the exercise book with PPAG pamphlets, all zeroed in. Her strength disintegrated. She lost control and took it out on Obea. "Shouldn't you have kept an eye on them? What were you discussing with your friends?"

Obea's face clouded. "School work, Mum."

"And what is that in your bag?"

"A book, Mum."

"What book? Kabria snapped.

Obea brought it out wordlessly.

"A text book? 'Science Made Easy'?"

"Did you expect something else, Mum? An exercise book, perhaps?"

And it hit Kabria. That Obea knew. She knew all along that Kabria had seen the pamphlets under her pillow. Her own thoughts earlier on echoed in her head. Their generation . . . things were different . . . they bawl out answers to questions still being formulated in their parents' heads. Suddenly she felt very exhausted. Creamy must have sensed it, because it responded on her very first turn of the key in the ignition. 'Thank you.' Kabria said inside her head. Had she been alone in the car, she would have said it aloud without shame. And so she patted Creamy's dashboard like a gurgling baby's back.

She headed straight to her room to change when they reached home, while the children sorted themselves out in theirs. And when she left for the kitchen to see to dinner, they also got busy with their homework. Abena, who always closed early to come home and get things started, had scaled the fish already. The stew was simmering on one fire, while the rice cooked on another. Kabria had had to master the organization of her household chores to maintain her sanity. She cut up the fish, spiced and salted it, and put the oil on the fire.

"Mum," Ottu called, approaching the kitchen, "what is this?" He was holding a storybook and pointing to a word.

"Spell it." Kabria suggested, and proceeded to carefully arrange the fish in the frying pan.

"A-B-A-N-D-O-N."

She pronounced it for him.

"What does it mean?"

"It means to leave something."

"So is it 'abandon' if I leave my story book here?"

"Not quite, Ottu. When you leave it and wish not to come back for it, then it is: abandon. Let Obea explain it further to you."

"She says she is doing her homework."

"Tell her I said she should help you please, because I am very busy here. I'll check it later."

He left under protest.

Abena was washing dishes in the sink. Kabria's mind began to play tricks with her, conjuring up images of a dead girl found behind a kiosk, who refused to lie still in her coffin during her burial day. Her thoughts ran wild. If ghosts sometimes observed their own funerals, like was claimed, how would a ghost witnessing that those seeing her off on her journey of no return were no relations and loved ones but a couple of grumbling city council workers anxious to get an unpleasant job quickly done and over with? She stirred the stew, checked the rice, and turned over the fish. Her mind wandered onto the day, which like all days, always began with work and ended with even more work.

A report once alleged that the African woman worked for an average of sixty-seven hours a week as opposed to fifty-five for the African man. So who really was the weaker sex? She called Abena.

"Yes Ma." Abena never called Kabria Mum, like her natural children. 'I like Ma better,' she had once claimed.

"Abena, do you know that in a country called Cuba, laws have been enacted to force men to help around the house? So maybe, by the time you set up your own dressmaking salon and get married, your husband will be cooking for you sometimes."

"Oh, Ma," Abena laughed coyly and looked away shyly.

Kabria smiled. 'How revolutionary that would be in Africa,' she thought, 'Except that whichever African government attempted such a legislation, would be gone overnight in a coup d'etat which, guaranteed, would have the full backing of all African men. It would also probably spark off a gender war, whereby sons would find themselves taking up arms against their mothers. One group of men who would gleefully fight this war would of course, be, husbands, when they come face to face with their mothers-in-law on the battle ground.' She laughed out loud.

"Mum, what is it?" Obea asked.

Kabria hadn't seen her come to stand in the kitchen doorway. "Oh! Just some silly fantasies," she responded, "can you heat some water for Ottu and Essie? It's cold." Then called Obea back on second thought when she turned to leave and said, "The exercise book that was under your pillow this morning . . ."

"I know you saw it, Mum." Obea cut in, "I knew you would go back to our room to have a look."

Kabria smiled wryly. "You saw me?"

"No, Mum. But I knew I had made you curious."

Kabria studied her daughter with a new eye and said finally, "Go and do their water. We'll talk about the pamphlets later."

Adade's car horn sounded at the gate about an hour after Kabria and the children had all eaten and bathed and were settled behind the television. She managed a smile for him at the door after Abena had opened the gate for him. But inside, she fumed at her recollection of all that long and easy talk about how if a woman wanted to keep her marriage always fresh and her husband all to herself, she had better make him feel good at home. 'Welcome him home with a smile,' they say, 'look good for him. Wear mini skirts for him if he loves seeing you in one. Pamper him. Do him this. Do him that. Gosh! Who pampered her when she returned home tired from work, only to go and continue in the kitchen while trying to explain the word 'abandon' to their son? Who met her with a smile? Who wore Levi's jeans and an open neck polo shirt, which she loved so much on men, for her?'

She took Adade's briefcase anyway, as he expected, when he handed it over. She passed it on to Obea, who took it to the bedroom. Then she followed him like a kitten into the living room.

"Oh! What a hectic day!" he moaned and slumped onto the sofa, "It's been work, work, work, Kabria. Just work. You cannot even begin to imagine!"

"Really?" Kabria said sweetly, with a sour aftertaste.

Adade failed to notice the sarcasm. He went through the ritual of removing his shoes and socks and tie and shirt and sat down behind his ready laid table. Later, Kabria accompanied him to the bathroom, and while he dressed and got into his pajamas, Kabria told him about Fofo and the body behind the kiosk.

"Where does MUTE come into it?" he asked, "Isn't that something for the police?"

"We have a role to play, too." Kabria responded.

She deliberately did not bring up the issue of Obea's exercise book with its PPAG pamphlets, in compliance with her instincts.

7

Kabria arrived at Agbogbloshie around ten o'clock the following morning and parked Creamy at the same place as the previous day. She came straight after dropping the children, so she sought a communication centre to call the office and let them know she was already at the market. And to also report that Fofo was as yet, nowhere in sight. Dina was out, so she spoke with Vickie, who asked to know what Kabria would do if Fofo didn't materialize. "If by the time I leave here to go back to the car and she is still not there, I'll hang around till noon and find something useful to do."

"What if she doesn't turn up by noon?" Vickie asked.

"She will." Kabria replied.

"What makes you so sure?"

"Instinct."

Fofo was still not around when Kabria returned to Creamy. She contemplated on what to do and pondered over where at Agbogbloshie she could possibly run into Fofo again. And although common sense told her it wasn't likely to be around the blue kiosk where the body was found and around where Fofo tried to rob her, she headed there anyway.

The blue rasta hairdressing salon kiosk was elevated about two feet from the ground on four solid iron blocks, one placed beneath each corner, obviously parts from disused vehicles. The space created by the elevation from the ground, had been turned into a rubbish dump, resulting in a haven for flies and mosquitoes of all shapes and sizes. Kabria took in the scene in all its clarity. Like the day before, people kept stopping on their way past to take in the spot. Occasionally, a small crowd formed, but otherwise everyone went about their normal business.

A crudely dug gutter by the side of the kiosk, which was infested with algae, stank pungently, betraying the liters of urine fed it each day. It added to the misery of the environment. On impulse, Kabria entered the kiosk. The inside was painted a lighter blue. Portraits of women sporting various styles of braids, decorated part of the walls. A massive Sony cassette tape recorder was blasting Kojo Antwi's 'Tom and Jerry'. And for the heads bopping up and down to the beat, it was business as usual – filth, stench and all. Evidently used to and resigned to the situation they found themselves day in and day out, the squalor neither shocked nor affected them anymore. Kabria couldn't help recalling to mind a story that a private gossip paper had once published about a notorious 'madman' around Accra Central whose regular reply to the question of what he was eating, was 'Fried Rice', yet it was always something from the garbage. This earned him the nickname 'Boolaso fried rice'. For the many years that Boolaso lived off his rotten left-overs, he never fell sick. Then one Easter Monday, a kind hearted church going woman, heeding a call by her church to feed the poor and homeless during the season, presented a fine plate of home-cooked food to Boolaso. The mad man consumed it ravenously to the pleasure of onlookers. Minutes later, Boolaso began hitting his chest in anguish. Then he grabbed his stomach, doubled over and threw up, emptying the entire fine meal out of his system. Kabria wondered if Agbogbloshie should one day be swept clean and the gutters desilted, and the rubbish mounds cleared, whether the regulars there wouldn't all catch catarrh.

She recognized the salon owner from her huge portrait in one corner. She was both a puzzle and a challenge to the wisdom of Mother Nature, who, when unduly interferred with, left in her trail dire consequences. The woman had bleached her skin from head to toe, which apparently caused our uncanny Creator to unleash His fury in grand style upon her. Having endowed the African with ample melanin to withstand 'until calleth' the harsh rays of the African sun, this woman, who had dared to interfere with the Creator's plans, ended up fair from face to ankle, dark at the feet, which refused to succumb to the dictates of her bleaching soaps and creams and purplish around her eyes and cheeks and underarms. She was a multi-coloured parody of nature's original handiwork. Her punished body found solace in a cute but pathetically mismatched sleeveless dress, while her stubborn feet triumphed in a pair of fine white slippers. Her perfume clashed with the odor of a skin whose entire outer protective layers had been gradually and persistently peeled away, while at her service to obey and carry out her orders, were eight young apprentices.

"Sorry!" she said, when at last she noticed Kabria, "You should have come earlier. We are fully booked up for the day. Can you come back tomorrow?"

In reply, Kabria greeted loudly, "Good Morning."

She gave Kabria a sharp look.

"I am not here to plait my hair, Madam." Kabria rattled on, giving her no time to recover enough to throw her out, "I am from an organization called MUTE," and stretched out her job ID card.

The woman got confused. "So?" ignoring the card.

Kabria put it back in her bag. "Please!" she beseeched, "I am here about the body that was found behind your salon last week."

The woman became alarmed.

Kabria didn't risk a pause. "I am here to find out whatever I can for a report I am working on. Please. Can you tell me something? Anything you saw or heard or know?"

The woman grew more bewildered. "Sister," she shrieked at Kabria, "have I done something to you? Do you know me from somewhere? Have I maybe snatched your husband from you?"

"Please, no."

"Then why should you come and spoil my day for me this way.? Do you live here in Accra? Or maybe you are lucky. You have somebody abroad remitting you regularly, so you chop dollars, eh?"

"No." Money men give to their gfs / wives when they fee each otha

"Yes. You chop dollars. I can see it. That is why you don't have problems of your own. Look," she gave Kabria no breathing space to interrupt again, "just in case you haven't noticed, I am here to work and make my chop money for the day. See all the apprentices too? They are all expecting something from me by the close of the day. On top of which I also need to save something to cater for my daughter. Her upkeep and education is all upon my head. So if you think you can just . . ."

"Madam!"

"Let me finish! You think I am here to add police work to my hairdressing job? My daughter ... oh! God!" raising her eyes onto the heavens, "I thank you that she is my only child. Thank you!" and levelling her eyes again with Kabria's, continued, "she is wholly and exclusively my responsibility. And you know what that means in these times, don't you? So don't come and trouble me this Tuesday morning. Don't come and make somebody's palaver my palaver by force. Not one cedi do I get from the man who fathered my little girl. The only thing that man ever gave her was his last name. It cost him not a pesewa. Yet he made sure that somehow, I paid for it. He came and quaffed six free bottles of beer at my expense. Six! Bought solely from my sweat and toil. After which he did the disappearing act from our lives, never to return again. So please, don't come and add to my woes. If a street girl's body was found behind my salon, so what? As for me, what should I do? Do I look to you to be the one who killed her?"

Kabria smiled. She knew on impulse how she was going to get through to the woman. "You know something?" she began impassively, "I am also stuck in a similar soup."

The woman frowned. "What similar soup?"

"Sister," Kabria began, calm as the lie she was about to tell at

88

the expense of Adade, "do you think it was for nothing that our elders coined the saying that: until you hear the plight of another, you think yours is the worst in the world? Why should I be standing here making such a fool of myself and asking questions the police should be asking, if not but for the same situation I am in as you. You were thanking God for your only one child? Sister, I have two to deal with. Two! Who both depend wholly on me. Two!"

The sense of solidarity Kabria was hoping for kindled like a candle flame in the woman. "You too was cursed with a foolish and irresponsible man?" she spat.

Kabria's heart churned for Adade. The poor man was definitely other things. But foolish and irresponsible? No! That he definitely wasn't. Yet, aluta, as they say, must continua.

"My sister, see my finger?" stretching out her left hand, "He married me, oh, after our first child, then disappeared, came back four years later, begged for my forgiveness, got me pregnant again and disappeared once more. And you know how it is with our tradition, don't you? Because he hasn't come to formally divorce me, I am forced to continue to wear his ring and stay married to him. Yet he is gone. And I have to care for our two children all by myself. Ah, sister, you have reminded me of my pain. Ah!"

By now, the woman was wholly awash with guilt. "Oh, sister, I am sorry!" she beseeched Kabria, "Me aaah, I don't know why I keep bringing up the foolish man. It's just that the six bottles he came to quaff at my expense … ah! What's the use? Forget it! Please have a seat. Sorry I kept you standing. Sit down."

Kabria took the seat, feeling both like Judas Iscariot and Archimedes rolled in one.

The woman did not let her pose her question again. She launched into her response. "To tell you the truth, my sister, what at all am I even supposed to know?" and shrugged.

Kabria broke into a cold sweat. Was that all that woman was going to tell her after she had so cold bloodedly massacred Adade's reputation? All for the sake of some information about a dead girl whose face she had never even set eyes upon before? 'The hell what are you even supposed to know?' she swore at the woman in her head.

The woman somehow read Kabria's thoughts and quickly resumed as though on clue, and said, "Actually, I didn't come to meet the body." And paused, waiting for Kabria to pose her next question.

Kabria didn't. She sat there boiling inside; struggling to suppress the growing urge to whack the woman across her discoloured cheeks. Did she think she sold Adade for such cheap and porous information? Then the woman spoke again. "If you like, I'll grant you some few minutes with my senior apprentice. She is the one out there in the pink blouse. She knows more."

Kabria sighed with relief. "Thank you." She muttered. And walked out onto the extended plank in front of the kiosk where some of the apprentices were seated on benches and in chairs, gossiping about boyfriends and co-tenants and plaiting the hairs of some customers who were seated on low wooden stools in front of them. The painstaking process of joining, bit by bit, the thin strands of long fake hair by inter-braiding them with the original on the head, always made a fascinating sight.

The senior apprentice, a large-boned copper-coloured woman of about twenty-four, co-operated with Kabria on the orders of her Madam, which were shouted across at her.

"When I arrived, there was a small crowd gathered around the body," she began, "People were arguing about whether she died here or somewhere else and dumped here. And before the police came and carted her away, something interesting happened with the reporter from the FM station. I am not sure of which one, but . . ."

"Something interesting happened?"

"Yes. At first, everybody assumed and thought that the girl was a kayayoo, so this reporter began to interview some of them."

"The kayayoos?"

"Yes. But after he spoke with two of them, their leader came and told them something. No one knew what. But after it, all of them became tight lipped. They refused to even talk to the police too."

"What about the two who spoke with the reporter before their leader's intervention?"

"They disappeared. Just like that," with the snap of her fingers, "Suddenly they couldn't be located anywhere around here. The police looked for them in vain. Then gave up."

"Do you know what they told the reporter before they disappeared?"

"Oh yes! Many people heard them. They said the dead girl was definitely not one of them. They know themselves very well, you know."

"So what conclusion did people draw?"

"The conclusion? Isn't that obvious? Somebody didn't want the kayayoos to keep telling people that the dead girl was not one of them. Simple. Or? Which means that somebody wants people to believe that she was a kayayoo. Don't you agree?"

"But who can wield that kind of power around here as to issue such an order to the kayayoos through their leader and have it obeyed?"

The senior apprentice shrugged and said, "Who knows? With Sodom and Gomorrah just across the street? Moreover, what did the kayayoos really have to lose if the dead girl wasn't one of them? Nothing. Theirs is to work and make money. And if a girl found dead here is not one of them, isn't it all the better for them?"

One of the girls called the senior apprentice and said, "Senior, what about the white fowl?"

"Oh yes," the senior apprentice remembered, "was it three days after? I think so. Yes. When I reported for work, a pure white fowl was lying slaughtered at the spot where the body was found."

"What happened then?"

"Oh. One of the market pastors came and prayed over it, after which a man took it away. Probably ended up in his wife's soup bowl that evening. It was a really fat fowl."

Kabria noticed one of the apprentices staring at her curiously. She smiled and turned her head shyly away when Kabria gazed back at her.

"Is there something else you can tell me?" Kabria asked the senior apprentice, who pondered briefly and answered in the negative. Kabria thanked her and went back inside the kiosk and thanked the Madam too. She cast a final look at the girls as she left the salon and caught them all staring at her and whispering among themselves. Then the senior apprentice said aloud to her, "Sister, it's like we have seen you somewhere before. Your face looks familiar."

"Me? Well, maybe somewhere in this market. I come here a lot." And hurried out.

"Ah! I am sure of it!" the junior apprentice exclaimed after Kabria was gone. "It was she. She was the woman whose purse was picked by that boy yesterday."

She prayed fervently to God that by the time she reached Creamy, Fofo should be waiting by it. And as she walked the distance, focussed her thoughts on the history of the two famous features of Agbogbloshie. Namely, the street girls cum kayayoos phenomenon, and the daunting squatter enclave carrying on its shoulders the disheartening name of Sodom and Gomorrah.

This was an area that used to be known as Fadama. So named by the early settlers there who were mostly from the north. Fadama means swampy in Hausa, which the area was. Then in the early sixties, not too long after independence, the combination of a severe flooding, caused by days of a heavy downpour; and a government decision to dredge the lagoon to fill the lowlands of Fadama, necessitated the evacuation of the residents to Zongo, near Abossey-Okai and to New Fadama, near Abeka. For several years, the area of Old Fadama, laid bare. Across at Abgogbloshie,

the government of the day, acquired the land for industrial purposes and paid due compensation to its indigenous settlers, some
of whom procrastinated over their relocation. Then following the
demolition of the Makola market in the heat of the 1979 revo-
lution, the pressing need for the creation of a new market for the
many floating traders, hastened the construction of the Agbogbloshie market, and the realization of the area's industrial hopes,
after the procrastinating dwellers were forcibly evacuated in police
and military trucks to new settlements at Madina. In anticipation
of the area soon becoming a brisk trading place, the Konkomba
yam sellers were relocated there from the timber market. Thus
begun the gradual settlement of squatters in the area on the eastern
bank of the lagoon and west of Abossey-Okai. Hawkers' sheds
began to spring up. Some northerners fleeing the Konkomba war
of 1995 came to join and settle with their kith and kin. The Accra
Metropolitan Assembly relocated there, the Nzema coconut oil
market, the onion market and the hawkers market. Simultaneously,
and as was akin to any inner city growth, the area's brisk business
activities and human throng to the area, brought with it, some of
its consequential vices. And in one of fate's most paradoxical
designs, while further in the direction of the Korle-Bu mortuary,
one of Ghana's most distinguished Christian church set in motion, their dream of a temple to the glory of the Almighty God,
this squatter enclave took an opposite turn. When or why or how
the name came to be, no one knew for sure. What became known
was that, in reflection of the vices that went on there, someone
decided to highlight that instead of whatever little good the place
may have had to offer and named it Sodom and Gomorrah. With
the increasing influx of migrants from the north and elsewhere in
the country in search of greener pastures, coupled with the consequences of the acts of some irresponsible parents which result
in children leaving home to live on the streets, the vices of Sodom
and Gomorrah gained momentum. Filth and sin, suffering and
ignorance, helplessness and woes ruled the days. And caught in

the middle of it all, were girls like Fofo who grew up never ever really experiencing what it meant to simply be a child.

Kabria prayed some more, and God above smiled upon her, because even from afar she spotted Fofo beside Creamy. But Fofo was slumped against the car rather awkwardly and her head was lowered. She called her. Fofo ignored the call. Kabria quickened her steps. "Fofo," she called again. And when Fofo raised her head, it was Kabria who staggered and almost fell back.

"Wait here," she gasped, "don't move. Stay still. I'll be right back." And ran to the communication centre. She called the office. Vickie picked it up. "Vickie," she puffed, "Tell Dina I am bringing the girl to the office. Something happened. Her right eye is bloodshot. The lip is cracked. The right face is swollen. She's been beaten up really bad."

They rode in silence until they were out of the Agbogbloshie area, before Kabria recovered enough from her initial shock to ask, "What happened? Who did this to you?"

Fofo didn't respond. She turned her face away.

"You will have to talk to me, Fofo," Kabria urged, "we can help, but only if you talk to us. And you need to also see a doctor."

"I don't have any money." Fofo muttered.

Kabria noticed her wince. She was in absolute pain.

"There's a clinic near my work place," Kabria informed her, "I'm sure my office will bear the cost."

Fofo gave her a grateful look and turned the face away again.

Kabria couldn't hold back what was on her mind. "Is it connected with your sister? The one who was found at the market?"

Fofo turned her head slowly to rest a look on Kabria's face and stated blandly, "My sister? Who died here?"

Kabria was baffled. "Was it not you who told me yesterday that the girl whose body was found behind the blue hairdresser's kiosk was your sister?"

Fofo put on a distant and unfocused look and Mumbled, "Me?"

94

Kabria grew bewildered. "Fofo, what are you up to?"

Fofo fixed her an empty look.

"Fofo!" anxiety gripped Kabria, "Do you tell lies sometimes?"

"Yes." She replied flatly.

"So you lied?"

"No."

Kabria grew desperate. This time she couldn't roll Creamy down the slope and simply vamoose. Fofo was right beside her in the car. And she was going to have to deal with her. "What do you mean, Fofo?" she snorted. "Are you playing games?"

"Games? You mean, my dreams?"

Kabria began to wish that Vickie or someone else were around. "What dreams?" she asked carefully.

Fofo took her time. "I dream a lot," she replied eventually.

"About what?" Kabria pressed.

"About going away."

"To where?"

She didn't respond. She only gazed at Kabria; then smiled widely and winced in more pain. "There's blood in my mouth." She said abruptly, "I want to spit."

Kabria obliged her at the next convenient place. When they set off again, Fofo leaned back in the seat, closed her eyes and began to doze off. At the next traffic light, Kabria stole a look at her sleeping face. There were faint traces of fingers; obviously from a vicious slap. Something about it gnawed at Kabria, the more she looked at it. But she couldn't place a finger on it. So when the lights turned green, she pushed it to the back of her mind. "One day, it will all fall into place." She told herself.

"Sickening!" Dina yelled, "Only a man with a low down soul would bundle a mentally ill woman into the bush and rape her. A stinking mad woman? Who is also already . . . Kabria!" she screamed, interrupting herself. And when her eyes fell on Fofo's face, cried, "Oh! My God! Who did this to her?"

Kabria filled them in on what she hadn't already done on the telephone and threw the office into a dilemma. Attempts to get Fofo to also tell them something yielded zero. She kept her lips sealed; winced continually in pain; and indicated that she was feeling sleepy. Then Aggie asked, "Aren't we obliged to report to the police?" And hell broke loose. Next they all saw, Dina was hurtling to the left; Kabria to the right; and Fofo was making for the door, with Vickie springing like a world-class long jumper, to block the entrance.

"No police! No police!" Fofo wailed. "No police!" and struggled unsuccessfully to get past Vickie.

"Why?" Kabria cried, as she sought to bring sanity back into their world. And all Fofo continued to scream was, "No police!"

Then Dina regained her composure and took control. "Sit down!" she ordered Fofo firmly.

The rest also found themselves obeying.

"Have you eaten?" Dina asked.

Fofo shook her head.

"Okay. We'll get you some food. And then we will send you to the clinic. Is that alright with you?"

Fofo nodded.

"Good!" Dina said; and faced her staff. "And now to us. Aggie, you will send her to the clinic. Vickie, you get her the food. Something without pepper. And Kabria, you remain here, and rest. You look like you just did a marathon."

Kabria smiled gratefully.

Dina excused herself back into her office to call Harvest FM. She got the 'Good Morning Ghana' show producer on the telephone. The producer listened keenly to Dina and said at the end of it, "I am sure Sylv Po would be interested."

8

"The pamphlets are under your pillow, Mum. I put them there this morning." Obea politely but brazenly whispered into Kabria's ear when she went to pick them from school. She deliberately stood waiting at where Kabria normally parked, and walked immediately to Creamy before Essie and Ottu even went for their bags.

The pamphlets were three in all. Something on PPAG's consultancy work; their new focus and their youth programmes. She smiled at the thought that Obea employed the same tactic she employed, to discover them under her pillow, because that morning, just when they were about to set off from the house, Obea dashed back into the house, allegedly to urinate. That was when she went and put them under Kabria's pillow. Somehow, Kabria felt a gladness in her heart that Obea had felt free and uninhibited enough in her mind to put the pamphlets there. But simultaneously she also felt inadequate about the pamphlets having come from Obea to her instead of from herself to her daughter. She believed in the good communication channel she felt she had established with her children. They expressed themselves freely in her presence. But on second thought, it dawned on her that, their free expression of themselves, was always only within the limits of what she perceived them to be: Children. Obea was moving out of that realm, yet it was as though Kabria felt so comfortable in her perception of Obea as a child that, she failed to see beyond that into the suppressed questions of her growing needs.

She went to the kitchen to see to dinner. Abena complained about her Madam at the sewing centre habitually sending her too many times on personal errands and causing her to miss out sometimes on some important sewing lessons. Kabria promised to go and see the Madam about it.

"Mum," Ottu came in, "I want to discuss something with you."

"Can it wait?" Kabria implored.

A surprisingly understanding and unexpectedly very co-operative Ottu agreed to hold on. He rejoined his sisters in their room to do his homework. Kabria also went back to the pamphlets in the bedroom and browsed through them. One generation to the other was sometimes like the horizon. So far away and yet so clear to see it seemed so near.

Her heart missed a beat on reading through the one on PPAG's new focus on the youth. From ages ten to twenty-four? Ten? A mother's shock with a reality of her child's generation. A reality she wishfully thought applied to other people's daughters; not hers. Just like many thought of AIDS. But then she considered too that the ten years shouldn't really shock her. Didn't the guest speaker on Sylv Po's programme mention sexually active seven-year-old girls out there on the streets? Fofo came to mind. Kabria didn't need to ask her to know that she had been sexually active out there on the streets. Dina took her home with her after close of work. The doctor at the clinic wanted to detain her overnight for observation, but Fofo grew hysterical about spending the night away from the company of anyone from MUTE. It seemed too much for her to develop some faith and trust in two groups of people within the spate of a day. After having lived without faith or trust for so long on the streets, learning to trust and have faith again was like a crawling child learning to walk. Kabria wondered how information like that in the PPAG pamphlets reached girls like Fofo, if at all. And how receptive they were of it, if it did.

"Mum! Can I come in now?" Ottu wailed behind the door.

"Can't it wait a little while longer?" Kabria beseeched, "is it school work?"

"No."

"No? What is it about then?"

"A cassette I want you to buy for me tomorrow."

Kabria's "Then wait!" came out a howl.

Ottu grumbled and moved away.

Kabria returned to the pamphlets. Something caught her attention. 'Youth to Youth Approach.' 'Peer to Peer counselling.' It made a lot of sense to her. Kids who did not have the benefit of parental guidance could benefit from those who did. In her time, PPAG was identified only mainly with the pill and condoms. The new PPAG and the diversity of their programmes overwhelmed her. Counselling and information on sexual and reproductive health. Voluntary counseling and testing for HIV/AIDS. Diagnosis and management of Sexually transmitted diseases like . . . Thoughts rang out from the deep. Overcome your inhibition about the issue of sex with your children. Jump the hurdle and race with determination toward facing it head on. Talk to them about it. Advise them. Let them know the joys and blessings of it when done at the right time with the right person and under the right circumstances. Be blunt about the woes when done at the wrong time with the wrong person and under the wrong circumstances . . . Where was it she had heard this? Did she detach herself from it? Wishfully thinking that, well, her children were just that, children? Had she been unwilling to overcome her inhibitions? To jump the hurdle and race with determination towards . . .

"Mum!"

Kabria gave up. She pushed the pamphlets under the pillow and rose to the door. She had to check on the food anyway. Ottu followed her to the kitchen. "What cassette?" she asked.

"Lord Kenya."

"I don't know of that one." Kabria divulged.

Ottu's jaw dropped. He was truly shocked at what he perceived to be his mother's unpardonable ignorance. "Gosh Mum!" shaking his head in absolute disbelief. "I am happy I didn't ask you in the presence of any of my friends. Everybody knows the Lord."

"Well, that is good to hear." Kabria replied.

"Except you, of course!"

"Except me?" Kabria shrieked, deeply offended at being accused by her own son of not knowing the Lord.

"But you said it yourself?"

"That I didn't know my Lord God?"

"Not God, Mum. Lord, the king."

"Of course the Lord is King."

"Oh Mum, you are behind times. I meant that Lord Kenya is the king of hip-life."

Kabria was truly hearing of this Lord who was king according to her son, for the first time. "So this Lord king, is his Lord, Lord, as Lord in The Lord is my Shepherd?"

Ottu felt great pity for Kabria. "Oh Mum!" and shook his head once more, "Yes!"

"And Kenya as in Nairobi is the capital of . . ."

"Mum!!!" Obea and Essie screamed together with their brother. Kabria didn't notice when the two of them came to join him.

"Ah, shouldn't I ask? Have you forgotten the saying 'If you do not know, ask'?"

"Okay Mum, ask." Obea gave in.

"Is he from Kenya?"

"Muuuuuuuuummmmm!!!!!"

"Okay. I'll ask from the music shop and get it for you when . . ."

"Oh thank you Mum! Thank you! Thank you!" they sang in unison.

Seeing their overflowing excitement, Kabria held back the ". . . I am ready" she was going to add. All three had apparently hatched the whole plot. Ottu was only the appointed spokesman. Which meant that if she wanted her peace of mind, since it was a battle with all three, then she might as well get them their Lord king who is not from Kenya. Her ears were used to names like Rolling Stones and the Beatles. Forget about them being British and foreign. Her generation in Ghana, those times, was as crazy about them as her generations in other parts of the world. Yet her mother, those times, also wondered why a group should choose to refer to itself as stones rolling. And asked once if The Beatles had any semblance to beetles. Her mothers ears, those times, were used to the tunes of the likes of Dr. K. Gyasi and E.T. Mensah and his Tempos band. A classic case of eardrums caught in generation tunes.

She returned to the bedroom and to the PPAG pamphlets again. Then called Obea. "Who gave them to you?" she asked.

"A friend at school. Her mother works with the organization."

"Is she involved with the peer to peer counselling?"

"Yes, Mum. Why? Are you very upset with it?"

"Oh no! No! On the contrary. I was rather wondering how it could be applied to street girls."

Obea was bemused. "Street girls? Where from that, Mum?"

Kabria called Essie and Ottu and asked all of them what they knew about street children.

"Are they not those who sell iced water and dog chains by the road side?" Obea retorted.

Kabria smiled. "There are others too." And told them about Fofo.

Ottu was horrified. "She doesn't have a home?"

"No."

"And no Mum and Dad?"

"Not in the sense that you have me and your daddy. They don't care for her. They don't buy her clothes. They don't feed her. They don't give her love. She doesn't live with them."

"Then let her come and live with us?" Essie sought a quick solution her way.

Kabria replied carefully, "You don't just pick somebody from the streets into your home. There are consequences."

"But you just said she is with Auntie Dina!" Obea queried.

"Yes. Temporarily. And under the umbrella of MUTE."

"But why should her Mum and Dad do that?" Essie asked.

"That is what MUTE wants to find out." Kabria replied. And said to Obea, "she is about your age, you know. And had her parents been true parents to her, she would probably have been in the same class as you. And who knows? Maybe even in the same school."

Obea pondered over that, and feeling the impact, snapped, "If I was her, I would hate my parents. Are they many, Mum?"

"The street girls?" "Yes. Too many. And even if it was only Fofo, that still would be one too many."

Obea digested that one too and said abruptly, "my Social Studies teacher said that John F. Kennedy once said . . ."

"Who?" Ottu cut in.

"He was once the President of the United States of America." Kabria replied.

"But they killed him." Obea came in.

Ottu was flabbergasted. "Who did?"

"Some bad people." Kabria replied, "Obea, you were saying . . ."

"Yes. Kennedy said that: 'The future promise of any nation can be directly measured by the present prospects of its youth."

"And so right he is, isn't he?" Kabria commented.

"Yes, Mum." Obea responded with a smile, happy that Kabria had talked with them, not to them.

Before she went to sleep that night, Kabria called Dina to ask how Fofo was doing.

"She is asleep." Dina revealed. "Fast asleep. She had a good cup of Milo and she was elated about it. I made sure I put in much of everything. Plenty Milo, reasonable sugar, plenty milk. But do you know something?"

"What?"

"For some odd reason, which she didn't say, she wanted nothing to do with bread. No tea bread, no sugar bread, no butter bread."

"No? Well, at least it means that she has started to open up and talk. Or?"

"Oh, yes. Not much, but she has given me some leads and names. Her mother is one Maa Tsuru. And she also mentioned an old lady called Naa Yomo whom she would want us to talk to. We'll discuss it at the office tomorrow and follow things up. I'm sure we will gain an insight into some of the ingredients that go into the making of a street child."

"I am sure we will."

"Oh Kabria," Dina went on, "You should have seen her face when I showed her to her room and the well made bed. She smiled so broadly that the crack on her lip bled."

"Really?"

"And do you know a final odd question that she asked? Whether I had a toilet under the same roof. And when I said yes, she couldn't hold back her joy about not needing to go out through the front door to find a place or to join a queue to go to the toilet. Can you imagine?"

"Hm. We really have no idea what these children out on the street go through, do we?"

"No. We don't!"

9

It was one of those MUTE meetings. And Dina was at her eloquent best. "Three days ago when Kabria had her encounter with Fofo and MUTE became involved, what each of us had in mind was the prospect of an addition to our alternative documentation efforts. But within these three days, so much has happened. We have become personally involved with Fofo, which has given a new dimension to this case. In all the cases we have dealt with in the past, we restricted ourselves within the confines of the purpose for which this organization was set up. We have established our alternative library services. We continue to document for posterity, information that one would not easily access in a regular library. We salvage knowledge and facts about people and places that used to be handed down orally and we document it. So that, today, we have here, such diverse and a typical data on unconventional issues like the birth of area names like Jericho and Bethlehem in Ashaiman, and the story of the stubborn man, who during the first republic, resisted his evacuation from old Fadama during the first dredging of the Korle Lagoon, till the last minute. Stories that are gradually getting lost because the human minds carrying them are dying and rotting away with their knowledge six feet down in their graves. A lady journalist friend of mine was looking for information about the evolution of an Accra area to its present state. She thought it should be available at the Greater Accra Regional office. It wasn't. She was referred to the National

Archives. There, she was given a little insight and was sent off to the Accra Metropolitan Assembly. They in turn referred her to their Sub Metro office. She was told there that in fact, that information was not properly documented. However, one of their employees was very knowledgeable about it and could provide it orally. Unfortunately though, he was indisposed. Could she come back when the employee was well? No, she told them. She needed the information right away. So she was advised to try the Department of Town and Country Planning. She did. And was told she could get that information only at either the Accra Metropolitan Assembly or the Regional office. She saved the energy she would have used to explain to them that she had already been to those two places. Instead she wailed for help into the passing winds. Someone out there heard her cry and sent her packing to an informal but very reliable source: two old ladies living at British Accra. They proved to be a fine pair of human libraries. When I heard her story I asked myself what would happen to all the other information inside the heads of those two old women. But today, Fofo has posed another challenge to MUTE. It is in a way, similar to that of the pregnant mad woman by the lagoon vulcaniser. But Fofo is something else. Our involvement with her has brought us to a crossroad. She is in our care and we cannot make her just another documentation case. A street girl who wants something from the government, who claimed a dead girl at a market place was her sister, who overnight was beaten up really bad, and who nearly bolted at the mention of the police. Yesterday she talked a little with me at home. She mentioned some names. But the question is, what do we do now? Where do we move from here? Does anyone have a suggestion?"

"I think we should first be clear with ourselves about what exactly we want to achieve together with her." Aggie suggested.

"Okay. Then let me ask you. What do you want us to achieve with her?" Dina asked Aggie. But it was Kabria who cleared her throat and replied, "Ultimately, her rehabilitation. While simultaneously getting to know what pushed her onto the streets. In short, her story as a whole. My daughter brought home some PPAG pamphlets from school and . . ."

"PPAG pamphlets?" Vickie howled.

"Well, I was taken aback by it at first too," Kabria conceded, "but after I read through the material, I learnt a lot. There is a peer-to-peer counselling programme on sexual issues, including HIV/AIDS. I would want to know how this works or can work better among the youth out there on the streets."

"What about the person who beat her up? And the dead girl she claims to be her sister?" Vickie asked.

"She obstinately refused to discuss that, but said she had nothing against us discussing it with her mother." Dina revealed.

"The Maa Tsuru woman?"

"Yes."

"And did she say something about what it was that she wanted from the government?" Aggie asked.

"Oh, that!" Dina chuckled, "She said something like, because it is the government who had the power to make people do or stop doing certain things."

"And the police? Aren't we obliged to tell them something?" Aggie asked.

"Something like what?" Dina inquired.

"Well, I was thinking that at least we should go there and find out what they know about the dead girl. And then decide whether to report Fofo's case or not."

Kabria expressed some misgiving with that. "Won't we be betraying Fofo's hard won trust in us? Considering the assurance we gave her when she wanted to bolt at the mention of the police?"

"Yes. But I still feel strongly that we should find out and equip ourselves with something about the dead girl from the police before we embark on our meeting with the mother and the old lady she mentioned." Aggie insisted.

"I think Aggie has a point there, Dina." Vickie came in, "we can call at the police station without necessarily telling them about Fofo. At least, not yet. Moreover, since we have decided to take it upon ourselves to go and look for the mother, won't it serve our interest to know something about the dead girl? After all, if she should turn out to truly be Fofo's sister, then she is the woman's daughter too, or?"

Kabria nodded in agreement.

"Okay," Dina declared, "so we go and say hello to the police and then go and look up Fofo's mother and the old lady. Agreed?"

"Agreed." All chorused.

"But what about Harvest FM?" Aggie asked.

"I am in constant touch with them." Dina divulged, "so Kabria, you and Vickie go to the police and then to Fofo's mother. I am off to the clinic to see Fofo's doctor. From there I'll pass the house and check on her and see to some other things too. Which leaves you, Aggie, to take care of the office and see about updating the two files: the mentally ill pregnant woman's and Fofo's."

The police station stood in a very busy area and was, simply put, a sorry sight. Broken windows, leaking drains, cracked walls and peeling paint greeted Vickie and Kabria. The officer behind the outdated front desk, who seemed very bored with his world, his job and his very own self too, responded to their loud and clear greeting with a sullen nod. Then after listening with a bland expression to their mission, pointed at a door. They walked to it, knocked once, and misconstruing a sound they heard as an invitation to enter, pushed open the door. The Inspector, who had been completely absorbed in his numbers and didn't hear their knock, let alone invite them in, snorted at their rude intrusion as he quickly shoved aside the lotto newspaper that was spread before him. He fixed them both a look to kill and bellowed: "Yes?"

Vickie and Kabria repeated their mission. He listened to them in hostile silence, then muttered with the wave of one hand, "Sit down."

They thanked him, studied the single seat offered in confusion, exchanged questionable looks, and sensing that the Inspector had no intention of conjuring a second seat for them, made do with it, with Kabria taking it upon Vickie's insistence.

"Yes?" the Inspector boomed again. He seemed to be enjoying making them see how very unwelcome they were.

"As we said," Kabria resumed, "we were mandated by the organization we work for, to come and find out what, if anything, has been done about the dead girl who was found behind the kiosk at Agbogbloshie about a week and a half ago."

"Bodies are found at all kinds of places at all sorts of times!" he retorted.

"We are interested in this particular one." Vickie stated firmly.

He gave Vickie a wry smile, cleared his throat, fixed Kabria a stare and snapped, "We are on it."

"You mean you are still investigating?" Kabria pressed.

The Inspector's face clouded. He obviously was not pleased with their persistence. "Who gave you the authority to come here?" he barged.

"No one." Kabria replied, "we are here to seek information for our organization."

"We work together with Harvest FM." Vickie added cunningly.

The Inspector sat up. An FM station? Just one mention of his attitude on air, and his reputation would be in tatters forever. "Look!" his voice took on a more co-operative tone, "Just this week we received our copy of the post mortem report. And filed it."

"Is that the normal procedure?" Vickie asked.

"That is routine."

"And does 'file it' mean something like, shelved?" Kabria asked carefully.

"Well," the Inspector shifted uncomfortably in his seat, "of course if something comes up requiring further reference to it . . ."

"Is it because she was a suspected street girl?"

That snapped the Inspector's last thread of patience. "Look!" he bawled, apparently giving no hoot any more about the FM station bit, "You think you can come here and teach me how to do my job? Do you have any idea at all what we go through here? We do our best within the available resources here. And as you can see for yourself, it is even less than minimal. So don't you come here and tell me . . ."

"Sir," Vickie cut in, "do you have any idea about the average number of lives that are affected when you are compelled to file a case due to lack of resources? Like the death of this suspected street girl?"

The Inspector didn't miss Vickie's sarcasm. He glared at her full in her face and rasped, "Madam, I know where you are coming from." And rose clumsily in anger from his seat, hitting against the edge of the table, what Vickie and Kabria now saw to be an enormous pot belly that was previously concealed behind the table. "Do you think we here are pieces of wood?" he bellowed, "turn around!" he ordered. And when Kabria and Vickie didn't obey instantly, yelled, "I said turn around!"

They obliged instantly in a daze. And while they sorted out their confusion he moved and stood beside them. "And now, look around!" he commanded, "Cast your eyes to the corner over there!" pointing to the right. "Do you see the filing cabinet there? That is where confidential reports are kept. And now tell me; what do you see?"

Vickie and Kabria stared bewilderedly.

"Look at it well!" he plodded, "Look! And tell me what you see. Think."

They got what it was he wanted them to see. The confidential reports cabinet itself. One drawer was so badly dented that it couldn't shut close. Another's handle was missing. And the third had a gaping hole where a lock should have been.

"I have been here a fairly long time now," he went on, "but I met the Inspector who was at this post ten years ago, one day.

And do you know the first question that he asked me? Whether this cabinet had now been repaired. Now, the furniture. Did I offer you both chairs when you came? Come! Have you seen my chair? Have you seen my table?"

The table was old and chipped at the edges and covered in scratches. And the leather covering of the chair was all torn up.

"And now pick up the phone!" he ordered Vickie.

She obeyed.

The Inspector's expression was one of cynical bemusement. "Well?" he snorted after a while.

Vickie rested a bland look upon Kabria's face and whimpered, "It's dead."

By now, they had gotten the message and wanted to leave. But the Inspector was not through with them yet. "Follow me!" he chided them.

They did, like two silly lambs, past the reception, to the front door. They nearly both landed into him when he halted abruptly. Then he pointed a finger into the yard and sneered, "See?"

Vickie and Kabria exchanged confused looks. They were not sure about what it was the Inspector was referring to, because the yard was empty. There was nothing for them to see.

"What?" Kabria asked.

"Look into the yard!" the Inspector repeated.

They fixed two utterly confused stares into the yard.

"Look hard!" he taunted. Then growled, "Did you see it?"

Vickie scowled. "What?"

"Are you asking me?" he pestered. "Don't ask me. Tell me. Tell me what you saw."

"But there is nothing there!" Vickie wailed.

"Exactly!" he grinned cynically, "You saw nothing, no? But what should you have seen? Shouldn't you have seen something there?"

And it hit Vickie. "A vehicle. You have no vehicle?"

The Inspector's cynical grin turned to a wry smile. "No. We

110

don't. Not even a battered Tico." And turned back into his office.

Vickie and Kabria followed and watched him slump down on his miserable chair, behind his chipped table. He inhaled deeply; fixed them a poignant stare and asked sweetly, "And now, if I may ask again, what was it you said I should do for you?"

Kabria looked at Vickie. Vickie looked back at her. They both looked at the Inspector and replied unanimously, "Nothing."

10

It is often written that, "No Ghanaian with money would choose to live in the inner city. If he has to, then only as part of an established extended family household."

This assertion was reinforced as Vickie and Kabria, directions on paper, weaved their way through narrow alleys and dilapidated buildings to locate the house described on paper where they hoped to find Maa Tsuru. It was a world of its own. Table top provisions shops were situated everywhere. A young woman with a cover-cloth wrapped around her, just above her bust, sought aggressively to sell them something from her table-top-shop when they stopped by her to ask for further directions. "I have everything!" she told them, "Even Heinz salad cream."

Several tables lining the rough potholed roads sold kenkey and fried fish with hot pepper. In every corner stood a crudely con-structed wooden structure that looked about to give way anytime soon under the weight of loud music and strong redolence of akpeteshie. Here and there, they encountered a lone man behind an old table with a sign proclaiming him as a watch or shoe re-pairer. The drains were all fully choked with filth and discarded plastic bags. Making out the house in the midst of the staggering disorderliness and congestion proved difficult.

"Why don't we stop over there and ask for further directions?" Kabria suggested when they spotted a compound house of about eight rooms painted a gaudy green. They entered. It was a kenkey house. One of two very fat women slumped on low stools and busily washing dried cornhusks under a shed to the right of the entrance was spitting venom to the other who was in a brown cloth.

"It was the second time he had beaten her like that into near coma," she spat. "The first time, he went begging her family that it was the devil that had made him to do it. This time, her sisters didn't wait for him to come and tell them who made him to do it. They cornered him, beat him into a pulp, went to him the following morning, and said: 'Sorry! It was the devil that made us do it.' Isn't that nice?" and roared into laughter.

Kabria and Vickie announced themselves, interrupting their conversation. They listened to Vickie describe the house they were looking for, and before they could come to mentioning the old lady's name, the fat woman in brown asked the other, "Isn't that Naa Yomo's house?"

"Yes, yes!" Vickie interjected.

"Are you after her?" The other fat woman asked.

"Yes. And someone else." Kabria replied.

"Then wait there on the veranda. Take some stools. DD eeeee!!!" the one in brown yelled.

A girl of about six emerged from somewhere in response to it.

"Go and call me your sister," she was instructed.

When she ran off, the fat woman in brown said to the other, "Have you noticed that I am not in a jolly mood at all?"

The other agreed.

"Hm," the one in brown went on, "as I sit here with you now, my sister, I don't even know if I am pregnant again or not. He is dead against condoms and won't let me use anything either."

"Ho! How? In this day and age? Why?"

"Oh, ask me again, my sister. He says it is wrong. That it is against the will of God."

"Who told him that? Is he Catholic?"

"Do I even know? Whenever he goes to church on a Sunday, it

is to a different church. I wanted three children. His stubbornness has brought us six. And he still won't . . . oh! You've come. Sisters!" she called Vickie and Kabria. And said to the older girl of about twelve who followed the six-year-old to the house: "Take them to Naa Yomo's house. They are looking for somebody there."

Kabria and Vickie thanked them and followed the girl out. They set off once more through the narrow alleys. And when after almost fifteen minutes they found themselves still walking, they began to think that either they had been way off course before they stopped by the kenkey house, or that the girl was taking them to a wrong house. "Little lady," Vickie addressed the girl, "Are you sure you got the message right from your mother?"

The girl giggled. "No one can get lost going to that house. Everybody around here knows Naa Yomo."

Minutes later she stopped at the entrance of a compound house painted blue and pointed at it and declared: "This is it."

Kabria fished out a coin from her purse and gave it to her. She thanked them profusely and walked away. Vickie and Kabria entered the blue house. Most of the doors of its twelve rooms were closed, but the front of each entrance was shielded with a curtain, which by themselves gave clues to the economic status of its occupants. There were fine, good ones reaching down almost to the floor, old faded ones torn haphazardly in places, and others that were neither good nor bad and fitted somewhere in between the two. The children and animals in the compound paid them no attention, while the few mothers, who were home, chose to mind their own business. Then one croaky voice made an exception of her self. "Whom do you want?" she growled.

They turned to the source of the voice and knew instantly that they were facing the famous Naa Yomo. They went over to her and introduced themselves.

"And whom do you want?" with a furtive stare.

"Maa Tsuru. Fofo's mother." Vickie responded.

"For what?"

114

And by the time they were through with explaining their presence and revealing that Fofo was in their care, Naa Yomo had offered them seats and divulged that Maa Tsuru had not been seen since morning.

"Do you think she is there?" Kabria asked.

"Does anyone want to know?" barring her last two teeth.

They were up against a sly old woman. "It would help us a great deal." Vickie pleaded.

She studied their faces, seeking to assure herself she was doing the right thing, and hissed, "If you ask me, I think she is there. She has locked herself up. They came looking for her."

"Who?"

She jerked up her head and frowned. Was she doing the right thing? Were the two women whom they claimed to be? And for two people claiming to be looking after Fofo, didn't they know rather too little? "Do you have children?" she asked them.

They wondered why the old lady didn't answer them directly. "Three." Kabria replied eventually.

"And you?"

"None." Vickie muttered.

Her gum smile reassured them. "I bore eleven children into the world, you know."

Vickie and Kabria exchanged looks. The old woman was obviously not going to give them any information on a silver platter. To begin with the number of children she had could only be the tip of the iceberg. They were going to have to sweat it out with her or leave there empty handed.

"Children! Hm." Naa Yomo rasped on, "Do you know how many of my children I have buried? Five. Eleven, the good Lord gave me. And five He took away. The same good Lord. And not one of them did I send out onto the streets. So do I complain about the five I buried? No! I thank Him everyday. I thank Him for the husband He gave me, and who became their father. He was a good man. A good man would never say to his child: there

115

is no food, go out onto the street and find some money for food. He would say: "There is no food, so we'll all drink lots of water and go to bed. Tomorrow is another day. You will go to school and I will make sure there's food to eat when you return home."

Vickie and Kabria listened intently. Naa Yomo was giving them a truckload of information. It was up to them to sieve out the useful handful.

"So where are your children?" Kabria asked, "Do any of them live here?"

"Oh no! They have all moved out. They are all in good employment. Three of them even work in other regions. Those who are here live in fine bungalows. They wanted to move me from here. Can you believe that?"

"You didn't want to go and live in the bungalow?" Vickie feigned interest.

"Move from here?" Naa Yomo screeched, "Here where I survived the great earthquake of 1939?"

"You were in this house during the great earthquake?" Kabria grew interested.

"Where else could I have been? From the time I could bath myself, I have lived in this house. Part of this house was levelled to the ground, but we stayed on. When they were re-settling others at Korle-Gonno and Kaneshie and Abossey-Okai, we refused to move. We rebuilt this house with our sweat and toil. This house was built on a foundation of honour. Now see what some of them have done to this honour." And pointed her walking stick at Maa Tsuru's door.

"What did she do?" Kabria asked.

"Do you know that this house stands on the original settlement of our forefathers when they came in from Niger country?" Naa Yomo circumvented Kabria's question.

"Really?" Vickie played along.

"Yes," Naa Yomo felt encouraged, "this very spot here, where this stool of mine sits, is proper Accra. Did you know that? And somewhere beneath this earth is my umbilical cord. The first two teeth in my mouth grew here. The last two would come off here. That was what I told my children."

Kabria grew impatient. Were they going to have to spend the whole afternoon with the old lady? "Naa Yomo," Kabria ventured, "Who was it that came looking for Maa Tsuru?"

"That man!" Naa Yomo got back in line. "I know it all. I know everything. Every morning when I come to sit here, I listen and observe. Day in and day out, in all these past several years, I have been listening and observing. I have seen a lot and observed a lot."

Kabria couldn't hold back any longer. "And the man?" she asked.

"Him? He came here. To her. Evil man. Very evil. And because he came to her, nobody wants to have anything to do with her. It's over a week now since he came to her, and since then, she is always indoors. But people give her food leftovers, because of the children. We are still family, you know."

"And do you know what the man wanted from her? Who was he?" Vickie pressed.

"It is the curse." Naa Yomo drifted off again, "I have seen the making of babies here, their deliveries, their growths. I have observed transactions, good and bad. I can recite to you the causes of many fights and quarrels in this house. I can attest to marriages, the proper ones and the co-habitations. This house was built by an honourable man, for his twelve sons. I am the daughter of one of those twelve sons. I am the only direct grandchild of the great man still alive in this house. Everyone else here is either a great or great-great or great-great-great or great-great-great-great grandchild or grandniece and nephew of the honourable man. I have lived through the making and painful breaking up of families in this house. I have born witness to mothers who cane their children into the classroom and mothers who cane their children out of the classroom and onto the streets. Thirty-eight years ago, she was born in the very room inside which she has now locked herself in."

Kabria brought out her notebook and noted down the approximate age of Fofo's mother. And asked Naa Yomo if the man who called on Fofo's mother was a member of the extended family.

"God forbid!" the old lady spat, "This extended family? A member? Do you know that my grandfather was one of a few Gold Coast men with whom the old governor, Sir Gordon Guggisberg, shook hands with?"

Vickie and Kabria didn't need to feign interest any longer. The old lady had hooked them. They wanted to listen to it all. "He did?" Kabria exclaimed.

"Yes." Naa Yomo bared her almost toothless gum in a proud smile. "And do you know something else too? As was told my great-great grandfather, who told my great grandfather, who told my grandfather, who told my father, who told me, my great-great-great grandfather was one of the early men of the Gold Coast who traded directly with the Europeans."

"You don't say?" Vickie proclaimed.

"Yes. He traded with them all: the Swedes, the Danes, the Portuguese, the British. Hand to hand. Guns and gun flints for gold dust and palm oil and even slaves."

"Slaves?" Vickie and Kabria howled together.

"Ah! There you howl! I also howled when I was first told. But so it was."

Kabria wondered what Naa Yomo's emotions truly were behind that declaration with slaves. Misguided pride? Who, in this day and age of Emancipation Day and Panafest celebrations in Ghana, admitted so openly to be descending from a Gold Coast man who connived with the Europeans in the slave trade? She began to worry again about time. "Naa Yomo, we can't leave here without having tried to talk with Maa Tsuru," she declared.

Naa Yomo fixed them a stare that revealed nothing and stated flatly, "Then go and knock on her door."

Vickie knocked gently and called softly, "Maa Tsuru."

No response.

She called again and added, "We are from an organization. Your daughter, Fofo, is in our care. And we need to talk to you."

Maa Tsuru still didn't respond. Kabria looked back at Naa Yomo. Her eyes were glued upon them. Vickie knocked again. Still, no response.

"Maybe we'd better go." Kabria suggested.

Vickie sighed. "Alright. Let's thank Naa Yomo and go."

They turned to leave. Then Kabria stopped in her step. "Did you hear that?" she asked Vickie.

Vickie frowned and moved back and placed an ear to the door. "She is crying in there," she told Kabria. And knocked again.

"It's the curse!" Maa Tsuru wailed from inside. "It's the curse!"

Vickie and Kabria exchanged looks, and knocked louder on the door. A boy cried. But Maa Tsuru went quiet. They knocked again. No response. "We are attracting too many stares." Kabria observed. Vickie turned. The children had all stopped playing and were watching them. The adults pretended to be busy, too busy. Snoopers caught in the act.

They returned to the old lady. "She is in there and crying." Vickie told Naa Yomo. "She and her son."

"Which of them? The baby?"

"That wasn't a baby's cry we heard." Kabria countered.

"She is in there with a baby and a four year old. Two sons. You didn't hear the baby cry?" Naa Yomo pressed.

Kabria and Vickie replied, "No."

Naa Yomo shook her head slowly. "She comes out only when she must, usually at dawn, to sweep, or wash, or bath, or empty a chamber pot. When a man like that calls on you, you become an outcast in your own home. Are you sure you didn't hear a baby cry?"

"We are sure." Vickie repeated, "But we heard something like a curse. She was crying about a curse."

Naa Yomo chuckled. "Would you want to sit down?"

They took their seats again. How could they leave and miss finding out what it was that Maa Tsuru cried about.

"You know," Naa Yomo began, "when the seed of a curse finds a fertile ground in a human mind, it spreads with the destructive speed of a creeping plant. And while it does, it nurtures superstition, which in turn, eats into all reasoning abilities and the capability of facing responsibilities. The only reason why my six living children are all living in their bungalows, is because, after the death of our fifth child, my husband, God bless his soul, stopped nurturing his superstitious mind and focussed more on facing up to his responsibilities. And that was why he died a good man. Let me tell you about the curse you heard her cry about."

Vickie and Kabria didn't need any further convincing. They sat down again.

"I was in the room when Maa Tsuru was born." Naa Yomo began. "And do you know something? Is it you who has three children?" she asked Kabria.

Kabria nodded.

"Do you know why God created forgetfulness?"

Kabria looked at her blandly and shook her head.

"Because of labour pains." And said to Vickie, "You will understand it when your time comes. You see, when Tsuru's mother picked seed with her, the young man responsible, that is Tsuru's father, denied the pregnancy. Worse still, he insisted he had never even seen Tsuru's mother ever in his life. This happened at a crucial time. These days, of course, puberty rites is considered nothing much. Those days, it was. And the pregnancy came just prior to Tsuru's mother and her friends' puberty rite celebration. Can you imagine? So for each single day that she carried Tsuru in her womb, she leveled a vicious insult at the young man. As the pregnancy progressed, so too the viciousness of her insults. Vicious insults. Yes. But still, well, just insults. Then came the day that Tsuru was destined to come out into the world. And her young

120

mother's anger at her young lover who had jilted her, turned to hatred. In that room, even as she saw from afar, death fast approaching to claim her in exchange for the new life she had brought into the world, she didn't soften in her loathing of her lover. A dying woman clutching onto the last vestiges of life through hate, she cursed when the time came, and cursed and cursed as she pushed the little life out of her. A piece of cloth was shoved inside her mouth . . ."

"Was she biting her tongue?" Vickie couldn't hold back from asking.

"No. It was to stop her from uttering more curses. You know how it is, don't you?" she asked Kabria with a knowing smile. "That moment when the baby is bent on coming and it is clawing the insides of you like ten thousand crabs digging with their pincers to break out free; and you feel nothing less than as though your stomach is being mauled by another ten thousand ravenous foxes … " Kabria winced. Naa Yomo paused. Then Kabria smiled. And Naa Yomo smiled back and said, "See? You winced. And then you smiled."

Kabria burst out into a loud laugh. "Yes. Yes Naa Yomo. You are right. God must have created forgetfulness because of labour pains. That was why I forgot the pain which was like the baby was pulling every other living organ inside me along with it as it was with my older daughter, and forgot the pain which was like a thousand tiny strings tied a thousand times over at ten thousand different places as it was with my dreamer, Essie; and went on for my third one, Ottu."

Naa Yomo laughed so much it sounded like a laughter stored up for years and waiting for an opportunity to be released. "All this pain," she resumed, "and all Tsuru's mother could think of was her hatred for the young man who had dishonoured her before she could be purified and properly initiated into womanhood. Even the sweat that spurted through the pores on her forehead as we all urged her to push the baby out, seemed to be in anguish to break free from their store house of hate. One moment she was screaming she wanted to go to the toilet, next moment she was yelling to be given a knife to cut her own belly into pieces. It was like she was being eaten alive by something. If you ask me, I think that in a way, she was. By the hatred."

"What happened then?" Vickie asked forlornly.

"By the time the baby's shoulder burst through her and tore to shreds the lining of her womanhood, the curse was on her lips. She was fading away, but wasn't going to go without a legacy. The cord was still uncut when she yelled that may her lover and his descendants after him, suffer in more ways and in more forms than he had made her to suffer. Someone shouted that she was dying. I cried that she should be made to undo the curse first. But it was too late. She lay there dead, while they took the child away. The child with no mother and whose father and his lineage had just been cursed. A child, cursed by her own mother."

"So Maa Tsuru thinks her situation is a result of the curse?" Kabria asked.

"Who knows? But something robbed her of her sanity."

Kabria frowned. "Is she mad?"

Naa Yomo took her time. "She has lost her soul," she replied, "only a woman robbed of her soul would do what she was doing?"

"What was she doing?" Kabria asked.

Naa Yomo said thoughtfully, "I cannot tell you yet. Fofo must know before others do. And Tsuru must tell Fofo herself. It's the only way she can salvage whatever is left of her soul."

On route back to the office, Vickie said to Kabria about Naa Yomo, "She knows so much."

"Yes," Kabria agreed, "if the contents in her head could be deciphered with a click of a mouse, she could fill up another George Padmore Library."

11

Dina was agitated over Vickie and Kabria's inability to meet Maa Tsuru, until she heard all they had to say about Naa Yomo. Together, they sought to sieve through the old lady's revelations.

Fofo was recuperating well in Dina's home, but was still not talking much. Dina revealed that whenever she asked Fofo a question and tried to get her talking, she would look away and ask of Kabria.

Aggie wondered if Fofo wouldn't have talked more were she to be with Kabria, considering their initial bonding.

"Are you suggesting that Kabria take her home to stay with her?" Vickie asked.

"That is out of the question!" Dina retorted, "Kabria doesn't live alone like I do. Fofo's presence in my home disorganises no one. It may, in Kabria's. She is a mother and a wife. I can't let her carry 'work' home so blatantly. Attending to Fofo requires extra energy. I wonder what extra energy Kabria would have for her after seeing to her own children, and food, and the home and her husband. We must not create a new problem in the process of trying to solve an old one."

"So what do we do?" Aggie asked.

"Eventually, we will have to talk with reputable organizations like 'Children-In-Need' or 'Street-Girls-Aid'. But before we release her, we must be certain she will be safe. We can do our bit by adopting and sponsoring her training and all, but we must tie up all the loose ends first. We are already too deep in it and cannot turn our back to the many unanswered questions."

"What is Harvest FM doing?" Aggie asked Dina.

"Oh! They are helping in their own way. Sylv Po will discuss the street children phenomenon again on his GMG show tomorrow."

Kabria felt like everything else was revolving round her. "So what can I do? What should I do?" she asked.

"It would help if you could talk to Fofo."

"Tomorrow?"

"I wish it would be today. So that we can feed Harvest FM with whatever new additional information we might get from her, for Sylv Po's programme."

"But who said she would open up to me?" Kabria wondered.

"She will. I am sure. But I'll double check with her when I get home. Then I'll give you a call to come or not."

Kabria was okay with that. "Then I'll pick the children home and see to the house and get ready for your call."

"And if Fofo agrees to talk to you, and Dina calls you to come over, are you going to go in Creamy?" Vickie worried, "Isn't it a bit too risky to drive it alone at night. We are talking after 7pm here, you know."

Kabria agreed.

"Then how about chartering a taxi to my place? I will send you home afterwards." Dina suggested.

Kabria consented.

On their way home after picking the children, Kabria said, "Obea, I am going to do something that I haven't done before. I have to leave you home tonight for Auntie Dina's place."

"Why?" they all shrieked.

"We have some work to do about Fofo."

"The street girl?" Essie asked.

"Yes."

"Is she still at Auntie Dina's place?"

"Yes. She will be there until she goes into rehabilitation."

"What work is it you have to do about her?" Ottu asked.

"She isn't talking much, and we all think she might open up more to me."

"And Dad?" Ottu asked.

"What of Dad?"

"You won't be home when he comes."

"No. Most likely not."

Kabria's calmness puzzled Ottu. Something that had never happened before, was going to happen. Dad was going to come home and not meet Mum. And Mum was so relaxed about it? "So what will happen?" he asked.

"Nothing Ottu. Why should something happen?" But it brought into focus to Kabria, how so used the children were to the status quo. Mum always got home before Dad. So Dad always came home to meet Mum. She chuckled. If even the children were that used to Dad always coming home to meet Mum, she thought, then how would Dad feel, this once, about coming home and not meeting Mum?

As if Essie was reading her thoughts, she said, "Mum. It is okay. You can go. If Dad comes and we want something that we would have asked of you, we will tell him to pretend to be you and do it for us."

Kabria laughed. My dreamer girl has spoken, she told herself. But what if Dad wants something that Mum has always been doing for him? Who would pretend to be Mum and do it for Dad? She laughed so much about the thought that the children joined in, even though they had no idea at all why they were laughing so much with their mother.

The telephone was already ringing by the time they reached home. It was Dina. "She is ready and waiting!" she divulged about Fofo.

And added, "Indeed, I think we should have thought about this even earlier. She is actually looking forward to it."

12

Given the option at a game of chance, it would probably be wiser for a player to have a go at guessing the age of a housefly just landed on his arm than to attempt to guess the correct age of a girl on the streets. Several times within the spate of the twenty-four hours that make a day, the harshness and complications of the streets can so hastily add to and multiply the aging looks and demeanor of a girl, and at such short intervals that she can seem like a child one moment and look like a full blown woman the next. The opposite was also the case when a child was picked off the streets and given care and attention, as had happened with Fofo.

The few days under Dina's secure roof and in MUTE's absolute care put Fofo through a tremendous transformation. She became relaxed. Her face was rested. She emitted an aura of softness. In the absence of the need to play the grown-up and the tough one to survive, as was needed on the streets, she looked and acted her fourteen years. Shyness had been non-existent on the streets, and Fofo had parted ways with it for as long as she could remember. But on seeing Kabria, she reconciled with shyness and smiled coyly.

"How are you doing?" Kabria asked.

"Good."

"Still feeling pain somewhere?"

"No."

"She is on pain-killers," Dina divulged, "and Afi has been pampering her a lot."

Afi was Dina's househelp. She had practiced her trade with Fofo's hair and braided it into a fine corn-roll style. Fofo looked completely different.

"I am happy you agreed to talk, Fofo." Kabria said.

Fofo smiled again, no longer at crossroads with shyness.

"Are we using here?" Kabria asked Dina, referring to Dina's living room.

"Yes."

"So," Kabria began with a smile at Fofo, "are you ready to talk? Shall we get started?"

Fofo cast a quick look at Dina, who took it as a hint and muttered, "I guess I had better leave you two alone."

"No, don't leave!" Fofo protested.

Dina and Kabria exchanged looks. "You want us all to talk together?" Dina asked.

"Yes."

Dina asked Afi, who was ironing in one corner of the living room, to excuse them.

Afi obliged reluctantly and disappeared through the adjoining door to the kitchen, closing it gently behind her.

"I suppose Auntie Dina told you that we visited your mother and Naa Yomo today," Kabria began.

She was seated in the sofa beside Fofo, while Dina took the armchair facing them.

"Did you see my brothers?" Fofo asked drily.

Kabria told her Maa Tsuru didn't open her door to them. Fofo shrugged and made a face.

"You don't seem too surprised." Dina commented.

Fofo didn't respond.

"We talked a lot with Naa Yomo, though." Kabria chipped in.

Fofo chuckled childishly. "Then you must have learnt a lot about her great-great grandfather."

Kabria laughed out loud. "Does she talk about him to every-one?"

"Almost everyone." She laughed. Dina didn't join in. She was dis-tracted briefly by a sound behind the adjoining door. She ignored it.

"So where do we begin?" Kabria asked, drawing Dina's atten-tion back to their conversation.

"In the larger sense, our interest at MUTE lies in knowing why people generally live on the streets. Especially in your case, Fofo, considering that you have a family home, and your mother is still alive." Dina posed.

"Yes. And you have some nice extended family members too like Naa Yomo. So why?" Kabria added.

Fofo contemplated briefly as though asking herself the same question too. "I didn't just get up one day to the next to live on the streets. It started with the begging. I was going out to beg on the streets, but I always returned home to mother in the evening," she replied.

"When did the begging start?" Dina asked.

"When I dropped out of school."

"You started school?"

"Yes." Fofo grinned proudly, "But I went only up to Class Two. There was no money. Mother couldn't afford the uniforms and the exercise books."

"And your father?"

"He wasn't around. He left us a long time ago. Mother said I was still not even born."

"To where?"

Fofo shrugged.

"So you started going out to beg because there was no money?"

"And no food. That was more pressing," she went on. "When there is no food, you don't wait to be asked by anyone to go out and beg. Hunger is a foe and it is overpowering. When it pushes you, you go. It was the same with Baby T."

"Who?"

"My older sister. She too dropped out of school in Class Two."

"Couldn't any member of your mother's family help?" Dina asked.

Fofo made a sour face. "Maybe some could have, but they didn't. Or maybe mother should have asked for help. But from whom? I don't know. Because most of her family members that I know, also have their children out on the streets. Many of them also had fathers who didn't stay around to be with them and their mothers. The best that some of her family members did for us was to give us their food leftovers. Naa Yomo used to feed us a lot. Her children brought her money regularly. They are all big people and live in bungalows elsewhere."

Kabria had an inkling. It just hit her. Her first encounter with Fofo as Creamy rolled down the slope in free gear. What Fofo shouted across to her and later denied in the car the following day.

"Baby T, your sister, what does she do now? Where is she?" she asked.

Fofo winced. "She used to say that as for hunger, you either took charge of it or it would gain total control of you."

Dina frowned. "Baby T said that?"

"She was always saying that." Fofo replied, "Especially when I was suffering stomach cramps and dizziness from it. Then I would suffer nausea and feel like vomiting. But there was almost always nothing in my stomach. So I would retch and retch and end up with a sore throat. Then Baby T would say, 'You see? You are letting the foe rule you. Take charge!' And that meant finding money for food through any means possible. Fair or foul. Begging? Stealing? Whatever. I learnt the art of pickpocketing from her. She was a very good teacher."

"You keep referring to her in the past." Kabria observed.

"Yes." Fofo admitted.

"Why?"

"Because she is gone."

130

"Where?" Kabria pressed.

Fofo frowned. "Do I know? To heaven? To hell? She was the one behind the blue kiosk. The body. That was my sister, Baby T."

"You said that once, then you denied it. Do you remember?"

"Yes."

"So what do you want us to believe now?"

"It was Baby T."

"What makes you so sure?"

"Mother told me."

"Did she tell you how she found out?"

"They told her. They killed Baby T, then told mother."

"They?"

"The bad man who attacked me. Poison. He and Maami Broni. The fat red woman who took Baby T away from home."

"When? To where?"

"Long ago. Before I moved onto the streets, Baby T went to live with her. Mother didn't want to live with Baby T again."

"Why?"

"Because something happened. Something very bad. I don't know it all, so I can't tell you. What I know is that I became very unhappy after Baby T was taken away. Then I began to think of what could also happen to me. That maybe something would happen one day and mother would decide she could no longer live with me too. Then what? What if she made Maami Broni come for me too? I didn't like her. And the more I thought about her, the more time I spent on the streets. And the more time I spent on the streets, the more its attractions lured me."

"Attractions? What else but discomfort is out there on the streets?" Kabria howled.

Fofo chuckled. "I led my own life on the streets. That was the first attraction. On the streets, I was under nobody's control. It was fun. The fun balanced the discomforts. I went to sleep when I wanted. I watched any film I wanted at the public video centre.

Whatever money I made on the streets, I kept for myself. All of it. And I spent it as and when I wanted. The time I used to go home to sleep, mother used to take my money from me. See? So as soon as I made a friend and joined a gang, I left home for good."

"Where was this friend when they were beating you at the market?" Kabria asked sarcastically.

Fofo got the message. She chuckled. "I got caught because I parted ways with her earlier that morning. Were we to have been operating together, you would still have been without your purse by now."

"And you would also not have been sitting here and talking to us by now. Where is your friend?"

"Odarley? She is still there at Sodom and Gomorrah."

"Do you know why she also left home?" Dina asked.

"She didn't leave home. She was sacked. By her own mother. She sacked her like a fowl. She said Odarley was troublesome. That Odarley was stealing her money. She is a bad mother. She just didn't want Odarley around after Odarley's father left her for another woman and she too found another man."

Another sound from behind the adjoining door distracted Dina briefly. Kabria also heard it this time so she paused as Dina rose and treaded soundlessly toward the door. She swung it open. Afi landed face down on the floor.

"You were eavesdropping?"

"I am sorry, Auntie Dina. I told Fofo something and I wanted to know if she would follow my advice and tell you."

"She knows everything already." Fofo came in, "We conversed a lot."

"So what was it you wanted Fofo to tell us?"

"The Househelp Agency, from where you engaged me, before I heard of them and went there, I was living with a woman who tried to sell me to a man. I was given to this woman by a relative of my mother who brought me from the village. She told my mother she was bringing me to the city so I could learn a trade while I served her."

Dina knew this was information that the Agency must have known but to which they were privy. They were not bound to reveal it to a customer like her who was employing one of their clients.

"Those Agencies normally do some background checks on their prospective clients, don't they?" Kabria came in. "I think they could be of some help to us. They must have loads of information."

Dina's initial anger at Afi dissipated. "Since you know everything already, why shut the door?" she told Afi as she returned to her seat. "I don't even know where all this could lead to!" she added drily.

"Oh, I am sure it will lead us to somewhere!" Kabria replied, full of hope. Then asked Fofo, "Do you always pick pockets dressed as a boy?"

"No." Fofo replied, "It was to disguise myself. I needed money to run away from here and didn't want to be recognized by Poison or any of his gang members. I should have left after you were gone. I stayed on because you promised to come back on Tuesday. I wanted to tell you everything. I was hoping you would help me. But as you know, the dawn of that Monday I tried to pick you, Poison had already attempted to do something to me. Because of that, I decided to return and be with my own gang too that Monday night. I didn't want to be alone. But it turned out to be a big mistake on my part. I should rather have gone somewhere else altogether because being with my gang, Poison's gang located me easily. They came to our shack. Odarley and the others were so afraid that they didn't even dare to shout for help. Poison is feared greatly. He is very elusive. But he has very many people working for him. They beat me up and sent me to him. He gave me one viscious slap and warned me to never utter a word to anyone that I knew the dead girl. Let alone that she was my sister."

"Why?" Kabria asked.

Fofo shrugged.

"Isn't it obvious?" Dina came in, "He killed her and doesn't want her death to be traced to him."

"But who would have gone after him? The police?" Kabria snorted. "A body found in the open at Agbogbloshie? A streetgirl of no social standing? Ten thousand people could be linked to her death and the question would still be: 'Who cares?' So what was Poison's problem? If he were indeed Baby T's killer, he would guaranteed get away with it! No?"

Dina considered that briefly and mused, "Or maybe that was exactly what he was trying to ensure. That the status quo pertained. That the apparent lack of interest in the body behind the blue kiosk stayed that way. He doesn't want anyone to become interested. If no one is interested in the body, who would be interested in her killer?"

"He attacked me to scare me into keeping quiet," Fofo muttered.

"Then hard luck for him, because MUTE is interested and MUTE will get others interested too." Dina responded.

"If only we could establish just a hint of his connection to the death. Maybe then someone out there who knows something would react." Kabria mooted.

Afi called Dina from where she was standing between the doors and said, "Wasn't Baby T staying with Maami Broni at the time of her death?"

"She was." Fofo replied.

"So where does Poison come in?"

The question was left hanging.

Abena was the only one up and waiting when, alas, the interreaction with Fofo over, Dina dropped Kabria home. Adade didn't wake up when she switched on their bedroom light. He was sleeping at the farthest end on his side of the bed. Kabria wondered if that was by design or chance, and tiptoed over to check his sleeping face. His eyes were shut rather too tight. Then Kabria noticed that the lids were quivering helplessly. She checked herself in time, or she would have burst into a loud laugh. That however, still didn't stop the 'Jezebelness' in her rearing its head. She brought her face down very close to his and exhaled a long warm breadth. Adade's eyes quivered even more wild and uncontrollably. Kabria had to cover her mouth this time to suppress the laughter threatening to explode. Adade had apparently been up and awaiting her arrival. Probably up to when he heard Dina's car horn. Kabria felt pleased and satisfied. But since he clearly did not want Kabria to know he had been up and waiting, she too would not let him know how it had pleased her heart. Let the marital game of 'snakes and ladders' play on.

She spared him the agony of more tempting long warm breaths upon his face and left him to drift into a much-deserved sound and peaceful proper sleep.

13

It was shown on television one Sunday afternoon. A film about the discovery of a young girl's body dumped in the woods of an American county town. The girl turned out to be one of a famous and perceived loose duo of sisters of the town. Interest in who killed her was lackadaisical. Attitudes were like, well, considering her character, 'hasn't she got what she deserved'? So investigations into her death stalled after initial efforts yielded nothing. But one girl, a one-time friend of the sisters, refused to let go. Her persistence eventually gained her the attention and help of the media. Through their combined efforts, the culprits were nabbed. They were the very two police officers that were tasked to investigate her death.

It was a story that showcased the potency that could be unleashed with a combination of the sustained interest of one person or persons in a case, backed by a media tool. Especially where for one reason or the other, the official body of persons who should normally see to it, don't.

The unabated interest of MUTE in Fofo and her late sister, Baby T, led to Harvest FM's Sylv Po becoming more engrossed in the saga, after Dina had updated him with details of their conversation with Fofo. Consequently, in agreement with his producer, Sylv Po began a series on the streetchild phenomenon on his 'Good Morning Ghana' show, using Fofo's story as a case study. His first guest, a Ms. Kamame, whose non-governmental organization had done a study of the phenomenon in Accra a few months before, confirmed that Fofo's story was similar to many cases her research team had come across. Sylv Po was prompted to ask for an outline of the main factors contributing to the situation.

"The obvious one," Ms. Kamame began, "appears to be poverty. I said appear," she went on, "because there are some very poor parents we encountered, who in spite of their situation, were not allowing their children out onto the streets."

"There must be other related factors then. Or?" Sylv Po asked.

"There are. Yes," Ms. Kamame agreed. "like the incidence of absentee fathers, ignorance, distorted beliefs and perceptions, and most depressing of all, the instances of sheer irresponsibility and misplaced priorities."

Unknown to neither Sylv Po nor Ms. Kamame, their discussion was beginning to cause a stir somewhere. For, just as criminals never missed a 'crime watch' programme in order to deduce the plans of law enforcers against them, so too did Sylv Po's programme, which began with a narration of Fofo and Baby T's story, attract some interested ears who proceeded to map out desperate plans to avoid detection.

"Expound on the issue of absentee fathers please." Sylv Po told Ms. Kamame.

"That is not only the father who refuses to acknowledge or take responsibility for his child, but also the father with a narrow perception of fatherhood, who sees his role as fulfilled so long as he has paid the school fees, placed food on the table and put clothes on the child's back," Ms. Kamame replied, "But the significant difference between the two examples I have cited is that, the child in the latter case, may not necessarily end up in the streets to beg in order to survive, while the child in the former case, most likely would. In both cases however, the responsibility of the mother doubles. She becomes the only caretaker of the child's emotional or physical or financial needs. Or all three combined. That means performing the tasks of two."

137

"Hers and the absentee father."

"Yes."

"It is bad enough for a mother to have to perform the double role of any one of the three. So if she has to take on all three . . .!"

"Which is what happens mostly in the former case. And if you are carrying a load and you begin to feel the first cracks of tension in the neck, what first thought comes to your mind?"

"Unload!" Sylv Po replied.

"Exactly. Which is what many mothers in that situation do. They unload at the first sign of any crack. The load here unfortunately, being the child."

"Like Fofo."

"Yes. Yet, in spite of that, look at what happened. Maa Tsuru went on to make more babies. Two sons."

"Which I find difficult to understand." Sylv Po chipped in, "Because the opportunities are now available for unwanted pregnancies to be conveniently avoided."

"That is true. But is it everyone who is aware of it? Or who can be bothered to put in that little effort required for the protection? Even considering that it also translates into protection against sexually transmitted diseases including AIDS."

"So what is the problem? Ignorance and laziness?" Sylv Po asked.

"I'll say ignorance and attitude. And if women who should act mature are not, can you imagine what is going on out there with all the immature but sexually active girls? But the question of attitude also has to do with one of the most distorted beliefs and perceptions. The equating of the essence of womanhood to reproduction. Let's have a little litmus test here. Who is frowned upon more in this society? The single unmarried mother or the childless married woman?"

"The latter," Sylv Po replied.

"See? Girls are pressurized to prove their womanhood whether they can adequately care for a child or not. You know the popular saying, don't you? 'You give birth. God will take care of the child'."

138

Sylv Po laughed.

Ms. Kamame went on. "In one of the villages we covered, it was common practice for a girl of sixteen and above who had no child, to be taunted and called names like 'man-woman' by friends and family members. Children have been reduced to trademarks."

"Which touches on the irresponsibility factor, I should say," Sylv Po added.

Ms. Kamame agreed. "Take our case study, Fofo. Where is her father? What about Maa Tsuru who has gone on to make more children even knowing Fofo and her sister were surviving on the streets?"

"That's the question. And what about the fathers? Why do many fathers refuse to care for their children, aside the excuse of poverty?"

"We came across situations where fathers were earning adequate incomes but were refusing to care for their children because they no longer loved their mothers. Meanwhile they had gone on to marry other women and making new babies. So you can see that . . ."

"*Hallo! Hallo!*" a voice barged into the programme.

Someone was apparently impatient about waiting to comment and contribute to the discussion.

The GMG producer scurried to fidget with some buttons. Sanity returned. Sylv Po announced that listeners wishing to call in should please wait till the phone lines were opened.

The leader of the 'interested ears' issued an order that the attempts to get into the programme should continue.

The producer had by then turned off the sound of the telephone so that only the signal button light kept flashing. Sylv Po continued without further interruption. But the continued persistent flashing of the signal light eventually prompted the producer to hold up a note to Sylv Po as Ms. Kamame began to say, "We met a woman whose husband had left her, after several years of marriage, with six children. He claimed he had a vision from God in which it was revealed to him that his wife was an adultress, that, he had fathered none of the six children. One week later, he announced another vision. This time, he said God had revealed the new woman he should marry, to him. The new woman turned out to be a young member whom everyone knew he had been eyeing since she joined the church. The man was an elder of the church. No one challenged him. How was the woman to afford paternity tests to debunk his absurd allegations?"

Sylv Po had by now agreed with his producer to make an exception of the persistent caller and find out what he wanted. So hurrying through the few relevant points remaining, Sylv Po asked Ms. Kamame about the vision of her organization.

"Our vision is to target our awareness campaign at those women and girls of our society who are more likely to neglect their children and make street children out of them."

"What about the men?"

"We are not shutting them out completely. But we recognize the urgent need to concentrate on the girls because it is they who get pregnant and who bear the brunt of that joint carelessness. It is the females who end up saddled with the child after the male has decided he no longer wishes to stick around and play father after all. So it is the girls who should be sensitized to this reality and urged to take the responsibility of their lives into their own hands."

"The phenomenon appears to be less prevalent in our villages. Why is it so?" Sylv Po asked.

"That is because in the traditional settings of our villages, cohesion and familiarity is so imbued in the lives of individuals that, women are more conscious of what they do. But in the cities, there is a fragmentation, which results in behavorial flexibility. A woman like Fofo's mother, whose 'village' happens to be inner-city Accra, is more likely to lose her sense of onus rather speedily when pushed by joblessness and poverty and the non-existent male support. Her physical and emotional detachment from her children is made less difficult in the harsh conditions of the inner city life. She let go Fofo and her sister out onto the streets with virtu-

140

ally no guilt at all because her psyche had accepted the situation with ample ease."

The producer signaled Sylv Po that the light was still flashing.

Sylv Po smiled. If the person calling had still not given up, then he wasn't going to give up any time soon. He asked Ms. Kamame his final question. "Why should someone like me with a job and a relatively comfortable life be bothered about the street children phenomenon?"

Ms. Kamame was elated at the opportunity granted her with the question to tell people with comfortable lives who think the issue did not concern them, to think again.

"You should!" she began, "Because the consequences of the phenomenon affects the entire society of which you are an integral part. Ours is a society where the family is the nucleus of our culture. These children are growing up outside the culture of bonding to a family. The physical and psychological effect of the detachment is to render them easily susceptible to survival through jungle street tactics and foul means. Then me and you who thought it was their problem alone, wake up one day to the rude realization that we have no choice but to share this same one society with them."

"Well said!" Sylv Po applauded. "Dear listeners," he went on, "from Australia to Zimbabwe, I am yet to hear of a child who asked to be born. If you are not ready to love and cherish and provide adequately for a child, why bring it into the world at all? Don't misinterpret me, please. I am not saying go get pregnant and then get rid of it with the excuse that Sylv Po said why bring it into the world if you are not ready for it. If you are not ready, don't even begin to practice what could result in the making of a child. Abstain! You can also visit the offices of the Planned Parenthood Association of Ghana. They will assist you. Ms Kamame, your final word please."

"Well, what I want to say is that, the street child of today, is being bred to become the kind of future adult with a psyche that has little or no comprehension of basic respect for human life. The question we should be asking ourselves is, are these the kind of beings we want to share our society with? So you see, it is not their problem alone. It is our problem too. All of us."

"Well said, Ms. Kamame. Thank you for coming to share your thoughts with us."

"Thank you for inviting me."

"Well listeners, I am sure that . . . "

"*Hallo! Hallo!*" the frantic voice barged in again, cutting Sylv Po short.

The producer apparently opened the phone lines a shade too early.

Sylv Po tried to make light of it. "Sorry folks! But these hitches occur sometimes, even here at your number one FM radio station. If my producer . . ."

"*Hallo! Hallo!*"

"Hello!" Syl Po responded. "Would you mind telling us your name and where you are calling from?"

"*Not important!*" the caller snapped.

"Oh! All right. But you have something to tell us and our listeners, I guess."

"*Yes. I have talk with you one time already at dat your FM station. Have you hear at all dat what I talk you last time? I not think so. Because today too, you have come with this woman who talk plenty plenty nonsensical talk and talk the same talk again. Dat make why I like talk to you again on your show, so dat all peoples can hear. De girl who die behind de blue kiosk at Agbobgloshie, her name is call Fati. She dies because she does something bad. Something very bad. She get husband in her hometown. Den she ran leave him and come to Accra. She says he too old. He too old? De time she was choppings his money gbla gbla like dat, dat time she not sees dat he too old? Now she comes take anoder man. Dat make why she die. She makes taboo. Woman dat get husband, why she must take anoder man? Eh? Dat not taboo?*"

"She had a husband in her hometown and came down to Accra and befriended another man?"

No response.

"Are you there?"

Silence.

"Hello!"

Silence. Then suddenly, *"I here still. Talk. I listen."*

"Oh, okay!" Sylv Po resumed, "I asked if you knew Fati. Did you know her?"

"Dat not important."

"Shouldn't that be for me to decide? What I deem important or not?"

"You say?"

"Oh, forget that. Where do you work? What do you do?"

"Dat too not important."

Sylv Po neared his wits end. "All right! I won't ask you any further questions. You tell us what you think is important. What do you want to say?"

"Dis makes what I want to say. Dat morning, I am goes to the Agbogbloshie market. Den I hears dat somebody have dies for dere behind de Rasta kiosk. So I too I goes dere to look some. I see dat true true somebody lyings dere. Complete die. Den something tellings me dat ah, I not knowings dis girl? So I look well. Den I look well again. Den straight, I seeings dat it is Fati. Her face makes basaa. You cannot look long even. Oh! I not think dat her mother self who born her can even sees dat dis be her daughter. But I know. I knowings for sure. Dat it is Fati. Oh! How she lyings dere. How her face all make big and big and puff-puff. Ah!"

"Puff-puff? You mean bloated?"

"Eh?"

"You mean the face was bloated?"

"Ah! Why? What make dis blo-blo thing you talkings me like dat? Why? You want insultings me or what?"

"Oh no! Please, go on."

"Okay. So me, dat make what I see. Her face dat make puff-puff. Den blood too. Plenty. Here. Dere. All. Oh! De face! I tell you, like not some woman dat come later cover her with cloth, like Fati was lyings dere bayaa

too like dat. No dress, no dross. Oh mankind! Dey has shaved all her hair too. All. Her head hair, her armpit hair, her dere hair. Sakora complete. Blood too. From dere. She bad girl; so she die bad die."

"But if you claim that even her mother would not have easily recognized her, how come you . . ."

Bang!

"Hello! Hello!"

Silence.

Sylv Po sighed. "She's gone, listeners. I don't know what to make of it, but I am sure we have not heard the last of this intrigue. Thank you for your attention, listeners."

Kabria was biting into bread and eyeing Adade who since he woke up, answered all her questions with either a nod or a shake of the head, when she heard the call to Sylv Po.

Dina was struggling with herself about what lipstick colour to wear.

Aggie's husband was insisting that the mark on his shirt collar was not another woman's lipstick.

Vickie was examining a new pimple on her chin.

Each of them rushed to their respective telephones at the end of it to call one another.

Each soon gave up because each other's line was busy.

Sylv Po who had been trying to get Dina since the programme ended, eventually got through just when Dina was about to leave the house for the office.

"What do you make of it?" he asked Dina.

"I'm not sure yet. We will meet on it at the office."

"Do you think Fofo is in danger?" Sylv Po asked.

"I don't know. But looks like someone out there is getting real panicky. Someone is desperate that it does not get established that the dead girl is Baby T."

BOOK TWO

14

The seed was planted years ago, several years ago when 'British Accra' woke up one dawn to the wails and cries of one of her residents. Those who rushed out to the scene, met a distraught woman who had sprinkled charcoal ash on her head and smeared some on her arms and feet and who was raining insults and threats on a young man standing beside her and trying to calm her down.

He was Kwei, her son.

The reason for the woman's action became clear when she cried, "Did it have to be her? Of all the young girls around here, did it have to be the cursed one? The one girl cursed by her own dying mother? Is she the one you should go and impregnate?"

The young man grew desperate. "Her dying mother did not curse her, mother!" he protested. "That wasn't what I heard. She cursed Maa Tsuru's father; not Maa Tsuru."

That pumped oxygen into the woman's flaming anger. "Stupid boy!" she yelled. "Stupid! Stupid little-minded boy!"

"I am not a boy, mother!" her son wailed, "I am twenty-three years old."

The mother shook with fury. "Shut your big mouth up. You call yourself a man? You think you understand the world better than I do? Yes. She cursed the baby's father. Your lover's father. But who told you she stopped there? Idiot! Let me tell you what she did. She went on and further cursed all of his descendants too. That was what she did. All of his descendants. And unless you have an out-of-this-world understanding of the word, tell me if a man's own daughter is also not his descendant? Tell me."

Kwei flung his arms in the air in despair. "Whatever, mother! Whatever!"

Such was the scene that greeted the young man Kwei's confession to his mother that he had impregnated his young sixteen-year-old lover, Tsuru.

Kwei was an unemployed mason being fed by his mother who therefore still saw him as a boy. That he had no job, but had gone and impregnated a girl, was not an issue for the mother. A child was welcome. It would add to the number of her grandchildren and make a nice impression in her OBITUARY when she died. But did it have to be with a girl carrying a curse upon her head?

She made her position clear to her son. "This whole family will have nothing to do with this pregnancy. Nothing!"

Then fetching a cup of water, she washed her hands at Kwei's feet and declared, "See? I have washed my hands off you too!"

Kwei was on his own now. He scrambled some money together, bought a bottle of schnapps, went over to Maa Tsuru's family home, and announced that he had come to 'show his face'.

Three family members accepted his drink on the family's behalf. An aunt now of blessed memory, a grand-aunt now known to all as Naa Yomo, and an uncle who ended up with the full bottle. They were grateful that Kwei had come forward to accept responsibility for the pregnancy. At least, he did not behave irresponsibly like Maa Tsuru's father. They wished him long life and peace.

Kwei's mother however, no longer fed him. His family also treated him like a leper. The peace that Maa Tsuru's family wished him eluded him mercilessly.

Kwei survived this situation for only a few days. Then he took the drastic decision to leave home. He went and informed Maa Tsuru's family.

"With a baby on the way, I must go away in search of work," he told them.

148

"Where are you going?" he was asked.

"I don't know yet." Kwei replied.

"How long will you be gone?"

"That also I don't know."

Maa Tsuru shed some few tears. Then she smiled when Kwei asked her to pray for him, and he pledged fervently that he would return with lots of money to take care of her and their child.

Kwei stayed away for several months. Not one word was heard from him throughout. But Maa Tsuru never went hungry. She assisted her aunt in her kenkey business, and for as long as she helped she got enough to eat. Then one day, the excited screams of two girls standing at the compound house gate, announced the unexpected: Kwei's arrival.

He came just like that, with little money and plenty bodily scars.

"Couldn't he have done a reverse number with that? Plenty money and few bodily scars?" Maa Tsuru's uncle remarked.

Kwei rebuffed questions about where he had been and what he had done. Then rumours grew rife that he actually got caught up in bad company that was into stealing building materials from construction sites in Accra's newly developing settlement areas. Kwei obstinately refused to debunk the rumours with a categorical statement on where he went and what he did. Maa Tsuru's aunt grew apprehensive with time. Kwei's mother quickly sought refuge in the matter of the curse and sang her son the 'I told you so' verse with glee. Naa Yomo cautioned everyone against laying out the red carpet for superstition in the mind. In the midst of all the commotion, Kwei wooed Maa Tsuru back with promises of better things to come for their son. Maa Tsuru continued to live in the family home and Kwei went back to living with his mother in their family home.

The room Kwei occupied was bequeathed to him and his older brother, who lived and worked in another town, but who was in the habit of popping up unannounced once in a while to sleep over. Kwei and Maa Tsuru may not necessarily have lived under one roof had they even been properly married. Their living arrangement was, however, more in line with the status of their relationship. Yet, Maa Tsuru got into performing other duties for Kwei as if they were a properly married couple. She would cook for him, send it to him at his place, spend the night there with him and return the following morning to her own home. Her aunt registered her disgust.

"It is bad enough that he has a son with you, and yet is obstinately avoiding questions about marriage rites and making you his wife properly. But you providing him with all the services of a wife so free of charge, is really rubbing in the salt."

The reprimand came a little too late. Maa Tsuru was already carrying Kwei's second child. He decided against travelling anywhere in search of work. What did the first attempt yield anyway? So he chose to rather review his attitude and to become more flexible in his choice of work. No longer would he insist on masonry jobs. He would do any odd job that came his way and that paid some money.

Maa Tsuru's second pregnancy marred her already soured relationship with her aunt. She found herself compelled to become more and more dependent on Kwei. It was tough for him, but with the arrival of their second son, Kwei's heart melted and his determination to care for them all doubled. For a while, it appeared that everything would be fine. Then the unexpected happened.

Unexpected?

Maa Tsuru was still spending the nights with Kwei. Neither of them took any precaution. They knew it could happen. They assumed and hoped it wouldn't. Then it did. Maa Tsuru picked seed for the third time. And their second son was still crawling.

Kwei became a changed man overnight. "How?" he yelled at Maa Tsuru. "Why? Why did you let it happen?" As though he played no part at all in the making of it.

"Nonsense!" Maa Tsuru's uncle yelled back. "Why didn't you

ensure it didn't happen by glueing an iron sheet around your loins?"

Kwei's response was prompt and cruel. He stopped Maa Tsuru from cooking for him with immediate effect, banned her from stepping anywhere near his doorstep, as he said to her, "After all you are not my wife!" Then he accused Maa Tsuru of being a bad luck woman and of having a bad womb that had no sense of judgement or direction. Maa Tsuru and everyone else were dumbfounded. Since when did a fertile womb become a bad thing?

In the secrecy of his head, Kwei also began to wonder if maybe there wasn't really something in the matter with the curse on Maa Tsuru's head.

Maa Tsuru weaved her way back to the mercy of her aunt, while secretly waiting and hoping for Kwei to reconcile with her. But all too soon, the pregnancy and the two young sons began to take their toll on her. She decided to no longer sit back and wait for Kwei to come to his senses. She called at his place unannounced one day to demand upkeep money from him. She did not meet him. His door was opened by a woman twice her size and endowed with a bosom the size of two extra large watermelons. This was most unexpected. Another woman in Kwei's room when she was carrying his third child?

"Who are you?" Maa Tsuru wailed, consumed with jealousy.

"Kwei's new woman." 'Melon-bosom' retorted.

"Who told you?" Maa Tsuru cried foolishly.

'Melon-bosom' in response, hurled with the flowing gusto of a volcano, every existing *Ga* insult, many of it, unprintable, at Maa Tsuru. Then crowned it with, "Foolish woman! Don't you know it was the curse on your head that got him into bad company when he set off during your first pregnancy in search of good work and money?"

Maa Tsuru returned home in shock. Unknown to her, Melon-bosom was not through with her yet. Like the cunning child who pokes a finger in a mate's eye only to run off thereafter crying to its own mother to lodge a complaint against the mate, Melon-bosom turned round and rushed to Kwei to complain that Maa Tsuru had been to the house and threatened to eliminate the two of them from the earth's surface through powerful juju.

Kwei's mother sang him another version of her 'I told you so' with greater staccato. Kwei felt his back against the wall. He took matters into his own hands. First, he shocked Melon-bosom by ordering her out of his room.

"Why?" Melon-bosom shrieked.

"Out!" Kwei yelled.

Melon-bosom scurried off as fast as her enormous bosom could carry her, wondering where she went wrong.

Kwei's next move got his mother rushing in despair to seek the services and fast-track intervention of a jujuman. He invited Maa Tsuru to his place. 'To talk things over,' he told her.

His third move got his mother acting and reacting. She smiled so broadly that it was like the elasticity in her lips had gone completely lose. Then she sent a messenger to the jujuman to demand back, pronto, her fat fowl and bottle of dry gin. Her messenger returned soaked from head to toe in a greenish liquid that had been angrily poured over him by the jujuman, and with a warning to Kwei's mother to come and appease the gods with another fowl and a bottle of dry gin for offending them with her absurd demand. When had a fowl entered a jujuman's abode and come back? But even this did not let Kwei's mother loose her smile.

When Kwei invited Maa Tsuru to his place to supposedly talk things over, Maa Tsuru arrived there full of hope. Indeed, she arrived there smiling. Kwei returned her smile and let her into the room.

"One minute!' he told an unsuspecting Maa Tsuru, and stepped out of the room.

While Maa Tsuru wondered what the whole drama was about, she heard a turn in the door lock. Kwei had locked the door.

Kwei headed off to his favourite drinking spot. *Agboo Ayee*.

"Two tots!" he told the *akpeteshie* seller.

She obliged.

Kwei downed it all in one gulp.

"Another two tots!"

Obliged.

He began to feel warm. He gulped down four more tots and felt his reflexes fairly sharpened.

"You want free minced meat to chop?" he asked the woman, wearing a strange grin.

The woman collected her money and waved Kwei away, wondering what he was up to.

Kwei returned to the house reeking like pure vodka on two legs. He entered the room with a bland face. No smile. No frown.

Maa Tsuru had just opened her lips to ask what was amiss when she felt Kwei upon her. He pounced on her like a cat on an unsuspecting mouse and began a viscious-pounding spree. He pounded Maa Tsuru with his fists, landing the blows anywhere and everywhere and on every part of her pregnant body. The daylight went out of Maa Tsuru. She began to bleed. Kwei grinned. He pulled her up by one arm, held her by the back of her neck and pushed her out of the house. Then he returned to *Agboo Ayee* and told all there that, with immediate effect, they had better start calling him Dr. Kwei, because he had singlehandedly and very cost effectively terminated an unwanted pregnancy.

Maa Tsuru's aunt refused to go anywhere near Kwei's home. Let alone go and confront him about what he had done.

Her uncle however, decided to be the man that he was and boasted of going to teach that Kwei man a bitter lesson. Then announced pompously, "I am going to get myself battle ready first." And headed to *Agboo Ayee*.

He drank a few tots too many, returned to the house and mumbled that he was going to change the blue shorts he was wearing into a red pair, because "My eyes are red!"

At his door, he stumbled on the short stairs; threw up as he went face down flat on the floor, landed in his own vomit, and slept soundly there for the next five hours.

Maa Tsuru for her part hurled every insult she knew, at Kwei, but from the sensibly safe distance and security of her own room.

Fate's machinery however, was back in motion with a surprise in store.

As the days turned to weeks and to months, Kwei observed to his utmost horror that Maa Tsuru's pregnancy was growing bigger and bigger and at a rapidly fast rate.

Never had something so singularly shaken Kwei to the core.

How had Maa Tsuru and the baby inside her survived his pounding? It must be something. It must be some power unleashed with the curse on her head. What kind of child then was it going to be that she would bring forth?

He did not stay around to find out. He bid his mother a nice 'Sleep well' one night. By morning, Kwei was gone.

He stayed away for only a year. Maa Tsuru kept appearing in his dreams, he alleged, urging him to return home. This time, he did not come with bodily scars. Indeed, he showed signs of having found some decent work to do while away. He was dressed neatly and smelled of no alchohol. He brought Maa Tsuru two half pieces of wax prints. Maa Tsuru's aunt's worst fears were confirmed sooner than later as she watched, from a distance, the effect the two wax prints were having on her niece. Then Kwei, like they say, 'brought himself one day', when he approached her, begged for her forgiveness for what he had done a year ago to Maa Tsuru, and solicited the aunt's help to woo back Maa Tsuru for good.

"Really?" Maa Tsuru's aunt asked with hidden glee.

"Yes." Kwei responded.

"Okay. Wait. Wait for me. I am coming." And disappeared into her kitchen.

She emerged shortly after, holding a saucepan in one hand and a ladle in the other. She set the ladle to the base of the saucepan and proceeded to produce the most unrhythmic, loud and ear split-ting tune yet composed.

"God forbid!" she howled, "God forbid that I should be the

one to hold my niece's hand and place it in yours. God forbid that, seventy seven times seven. I have washed my hands off the two of you!" And wrung her hands in the air with great fury.

Kwei gave up on that angle and approached it from the uncle's, with a bottle of imported schnapps. He added some money and promised that he would come back in a few days' time to discuss the marriage ceremony.

Kwei and Maa Tsuru's first daughter, but third child, who was born during Kwei's unceremonious absence, was never honoured with a Kwei family name at birth. She went first by the name 'Tsuru's baby'; which evolved to 'Baby Tsuru'; and then, to 'Baby T'.

Much to the displeasure and heartache of her aunt, Maa Tsuru started cooking for Kwei again and took to sleeping over at his place. Kwei did not 'glue an iron sheet around his loins'. One morning, Kwei's mother summoned him.

"Twice in the past, I woke up in the morning and you were gone. This time, it is I asking you to go. Go! Kwei, go! Go far away from here. The number 'five' has always been in conflict with the spirit of this family. She is carrying your fourth child. Have you noticed? I shall not sit down idly and watch you go on to make a fifth child with her. I shall not allow you to bring such calamity to bear on this family. So go away. It is the only way to keep you from her. Go away. And this time, please, stay away for good. For the sake of us all."

Two superstitious swords crossed paths. A cursed woman and the number five? It was time to escape. He had done enough harm to himself already. He had bedevilled his family enough through mixing blood four whole times with Maa Tsuru. Five times would be provoking the spirits of his family. It would be throwing a challenge to them to prove their potency. Doom would befall them all.

Superstition found a fertile ground in another mind. Responsibility needed no longer be faced up to. Everything could be blamed on the curse. Kwei was beyond being swayed. Not by anyone, and not by his own self. Maa Tsuru was too fertile, and it was a curse. It was the curse that made her pick seed whenever he touched her. Overfertility, even in a society where infertility was the curse of curses, could be as bad an omen as infertility. It was the most twisted of twisted fates.

Maa Tsuru had not the slightest idea about where Kwei was when she neared her term. She had no idea if he was dead or alive, when she gave birth to their second daughter, their fourth child. Kwei's family yet again did not honour the baby with a name. She could not also be called Tsuru's baby. Not even Tsuru's baby number two, even if the older one eventually evolved into Baby T. She ended up with the name Fofo. Someone decided that she looked like an old relative by that name. No one objected, so Fofo stuck.

By the time Fofo's two older brothers each struck ten, they were running errands at the seaside and the fish market. Baby T and Fofo by then were performing petty chores for family members in exchange for food leftovers and old clothes.

Kwei was gone, but his lover and their children remained together. Every evening, after their errands, the boys returned home to spend the night and be with their mother and two young sisters. They were poor, but they were together.

Then the unexpected happened.

15

He had been staying in the family house for as long as they could remember, because he was there before any of them were born.

He was the son of one of Naa Yomo's cousins; and he was a kind man.

The curtain hanging in front of his door was clear indication that he was one of the few better offs in the compound house. He owned a colour television that was in excellent condition and a big cassette tape recorder, which was an original, made in Japan. He wasn't married, but had made two sons with two different women, each of whom lived in their own respective family homes. The kids in the house often fought among themselves to run errands for him because he tipped well. He was a generous man. And the children liked him even more because he always allowed them into his room to watch television. He was like an uncle to everyone. The children saw him as such, and corrupted Uncle into Onko. The young and the old all called him, Onko. He was known to always have toffees in his room to soothe and calm down crying children. Many of them found it easier to talk to him than to their own fathers. He took good care of his two sons and their mothers but he never allowed any of them to come and live with him.

Fofo and Baby T turned to Onko in their confusion when after

157

having become used to growing up with their mother and two older brothers alone, a man suddenly joined them one day in their one room and Maa Tsuru told them to look upon him as their new father.

Maa Tsuru had been without a man since Kwei disappeared from their lives. She wasn't in any regular job either. Following the death of her aunt in whose kenkey business she was employed, she only contended herself with odd jobs now and then. She would work a few days at a kenkey house or do people's washing for a fee. She never stayed on one job for long because her two sons kept them going with the money and free fish they brought in daily from the seaside and the fish market. Fofo and Baby T were also bringing home money from the streets. It wasn't living, but they were surviving fairly well.

One afternoon, while returning from a house where she had gone to collect dirty clothes for washing the following dawn, a man who had been trying for some time to gain her attention, eventually did. For the next few days, they met regularly to finetune their growing relationship. He wasn't working. She knew it because he told her. It didn't bother her much because he assured her that it was only temporary.

"I work with an aluminium factory in Tema," he told her. "Have you heard of that big factory that had to shut down briefly two weeks ago for rehabilitation works?"

Maa Tsuru hadn't and told him so.

"Ah, its not important!" he waved off her ignorance. "Just don't worry. It is only for some few months. Some big white people have come from Europe and America to rehabilitate the place. It was built as far back as in Kwame Nkrumah's time and has never seen any rehabilitation before. Can you believe that?"

Maa Tsuru smiled.

"Anyway," he went on, "As soon as they finish, they will call us all back. Then I, Nii Kpakpo, would be able to take good care of you."

158

Maa Tsuru believed him. He gave her no cause not to. She reached out in her heart to him. So much so that she didn't even question his decision that she never visited him at his home. He gave her a good reason for it.

"You know how everyone around here feel about the curse on your head, don't you?" he asked her. "My family is no exception. They will not take kindly to our relationship. So I will be visiting you."

That became the routine.

With his factory allegedly undergoing rehabilitation, Kpakpo had plenty of time on hand for visiting. He visited Maa Tsuru regularly, mostly in the afternoons, when Fofo and Baby T were out on the streets and the boys were gone to the seaside and the fish market.

When Kpakpo visited, Maa Tsuru cooked for him to eat. After all, he was temporarily out of work. From where was he to get money to contribute to his feeding?

Since food was guaranteed whenever he visited, Kpakpo established regular afternoon calls on Maa Tsuru. Man, moreover, shall not live by bread alone, no? So one afternoon when he set off to her place, he stopped by *Agboo Ayee*. He quaffed two tots of '*Kill-me-quick*' for the '*Talk what's on your mind to your mother-in-law*' effect. Then another two tots of '*bitters*' for the aphrodisiac effect. He arrived at Maa Tsuru's, prepared to do *Cupid's* battle. He was not sure of what her reaction would be. One could never be sure with women. If the risk he was about to take should annoy her, he might find himself having to say an unexpected and unplanned *adieu* to his regular free lunches. Better whack the kenkey and fish gravy first, and then take the risk.

He did; topped it with three plastic cups of water and removed the pieces of fish remnants stuck between his teeth with his little fingernail. Then wearing the most tender of looks he could muster under the circumstances, for Maa Tsuru, he moaned, "I miss sharing the same bed with you at night, Tsuru."

He got more than he had bargained for. Not only did Maa Tsuru not get angry at all as he had remotely feared, but she actually felt flattered by it. Kpakpo was desirous to retire to bed with her at night and wake up with her in the morning?

The following day she went to the Agbogbloshie railways and bought secondhand curtains.

Previously, she used to sleep on the bed. Fofo and Baby T slept on mats on the floor beside the bed, while their older brothers slept on mats further away towards the door.

With their new father, Kpakpo, now moving in with them, Maa Tsuru divided the room into a 'chamber' and a 'hall' with the curtains she had bought. Then she ordered Fofo and Baby T out of their old sleeping place, which was now part of the chamber, to join their brothers at the part that was now the hall.

The first night with their new father in the room, the boys did not sleep for one second. The lights were off in the room but the outside light seeped through the spaces of the wooden window. And the curtain was translucent. They were early risers, which was norm with them because work at the seaside demanded it. So their absence when the rest woke up caused no uproar. Then the emptiness in one corner of the room caught their attention. It had been where the two bags containing the few belongings of the boys had been sitting.

Maa Tsuru could have gone to look for her sons. She decided not to. She had noticed them toss and turn on their mats the whole night through. They saw it all. For how long could that go on? Better let them go. They were no longer kids. The streets had accelerated their growth. It was time for them to be on their own.

There was a price waiting to be paid, which Maa Tsuru did not take into consideration.

The boys were gone with their contribution to the daily household income. Maa Tsuru began to feel the pinch. She dropped a hint to Kpakpo, but either he did not get it, or he refused to get it. Sleep began to elude Maa Tsuru. She reacted typically, by becoming suspicious, which common sense should have made her become from the onset. She did what she should have done a long time before. Nose around. Her worst fears hit her straight in the face. Kpakpo was no worker in a factory at Tema. He had been out of work for so long a time that no one even remembered any longer when he last worked. Or if indeed, he ever did. He had been surviving through dubious means. Accra was overflowing with desperate single men and women looking for cheap accommodation, so there was always someone to dupe. He would demand rent advance from a prospective tenant with a view to renting out his one room at his family house in central Accra to the person. When the cash landed safe and sound in his hand, pop, comes his 'Tenancy Agreement'. Unwritten. It was always the same verbal one condition and one condition only. The landlord's right and priviledge to 'perch' with the tenant throughout the period of tenancy. None of the tenants who passed through his noose ever succeeded in collecting back what money they paid Kpakpo. Some gave up, never moving in with him. Others moved in with him, stayed briefly, gave up and moved out. The tenant before the existing one was a man from whom Kpakpo collected two years advance and who decided to sweat it out with him. He lasted a year, the worst one-year of his entire life. Kpakpo literally imported hell from down under into the room.

Every night, Kpakpo returned late from town reeking of the worst kind of *Akpeteshie*. While asleep, he claimed he always dreamt he was a pregnant woman feeling nauseous. He would spit on end throughout the night all over the one tiny stuffy room, not caring about what volume he spat out, or its 'aroma', or where it landed. The man could never sleep well. He had to always remain half awake and alert, just in case Kpakpo would clear his throat, ready to spew out the stinky sticky contents from his mouth, because unless he yelled or kicked or hit him into full awakenment, Kpakpo always landed the product of his bizarre dream on his bed, beside it, or as happened once, and thank God for that, right upon his forehead. The man threw in the towel after one year and prayed to God for justice to be done. God must have apparently been wide awake at the time of his prayer because He heard him on the fast track lane. Kpakpo's next tenant turned out to be a court bailiff who had a brother who was a police constable and another brother who was a corporal in the army. The new tenant disclosed all these to Kpakpo only after he had paid Kpakpo the two years advance and Kpakpo had squandered it. Then together with his two brothers, each of them wearing their respective uniforms, they came and issued a stern warning and an ultimatum to Kpakpo to vamoose from the room with immediate effect. Kpakpo took a good look at all three and realized in time that he would be playing with fire not to oblige. The end had come.

From one moment to the next, Kpakpo became a floating one-room landlord without accommodation. Maa Tsuru became his covenient and readily available solution.

All who thought that Maa Tsuru would get rid of Kpakpo after the truth about him came out were to be disappointed. She didn't. It turned out that she was pregnant with his first child. Kpakpo still did not have a job. Maa Tsuru continued to do odd jobs now and then. Baby T and Fofo added whatever they made off the streets. Two months from full term, Maa Tsuru went into premature labour one evening. She was detained overnight at the midwife's. For the first time, Baby T and Fofo had to sleep in the room alone with their new father, Kpakpo. They were watching television in Onko's room with other children when Kpakpo came and summoned them to bed. For once he was not drunk. If they did not follow him, he would lock them out, he threatened. Reluctantly, they rose and followed him.

It wasn't quite a dream; nor was it a sound. It was more like her guardian angel whispering into her ears. Fofo woke up. She lay there quiet; her eyes opened. She did not raise her head. She watched.

162

Kpakpo tiptoed over to Baby T and tapped her on the shoulder. Baby T sprang up, still drowsy. Kpakpo beckoned her to follow him. It all seemed like a scene in a zombie film. Baby T rose. Kpakpo beckoned again, impatiently, forcefully. Baby T walked slowly, like there was no life in her. She followed him to behind the curtain. Fofo's heart pounded fast and loud inside her chest. It was like it would burst and hurl itself out through her chest. Kpakpo took Baby T's hand and sat on the bed. He placed Baby T before him and signaled her to remove her dress. Baby T obeyed as though in a trance. He savoured Baby T's maturing body hungrily with his eyes. Then he brushed the back of one hand over Baby T's breasts and drew down her pants. They fell to the floor. Baby T stepped out of them mechanically. She didn't wait to be told. Kpakpo held the back of her tiny lower waist with one hand and placed the other hand between Baby T's thighs. Fofo shook lightly. Then as she watched Baby T being guided onto the bed by their new father, she shook violently. Kpakpo stripped naked in frenzy, filled with an urgency so wrong by Baby T's nakedness. Fofo's quivering muscles generated a current flow. It shocked her into stillness as Baby T disappeared wholly and completely beneath him, covered entirely even by his relatively small frame. Fofo shut her eyes tight. She kept them tightly shut, Onko on her mind. Onko the kind man. Onko the generous and understanding man. She would go and unburden her confusion upon Onko's shoulders in the morning. She began to rehearse inside her head how she would go about breaking the news to Onko. Somewhere along the line, she surrendered to unconsciousness and drifted to sleep.

Baby T was beside her on the floor mat when she woke up. All Fofo could do was stare blankly at her sister. Baby T stared back from a depth deep and unreachable. Then Baby T read the lingering question crying to be answered, in Fofo's eyes.

"He didn't do it!" she muttered. Her voice sounded like coming from outside of her. "He touched me with his fingers," she went on, "He got on top of me. He was going to do it. Then he stopped. All of a sudden he stopped. Something stopped him. So he didn't do it."

Fofo stared at her sister with eyes that seemed not to actually see. Then she turned her face away slowly and resumed going over inside her head how she would break the news to Onko.

Onko would know what to do. Onko would know the right thing to do.

Maa Tsuru returned home without a baby the following day. It had been stillborn.

The gossip reached her ears the very minute she landed in the house. She played deaf to it and resumed life with Kpakpo from where she left off.

One morning several days later, Fofo came and lodged a report.

"Mother, Baby T is sitting at the edge of the gutter."

"Which gutter?"

"The one behind the house."

"Doing what?"

"Nothing. She is just sitting there and shivering. I touched her forehead. She is very very hot."

'Paracetamol' echoed in Maa Tsuru's head. "Go and call her for me!" she ordered Fofo.

Fofo pretended not to have heard.

"I said go and call her for me!" Maa Tsuru yelled. "Then come for some money for some *para* for her."

Fofo wore a sullen look, took two steps and stopped.

A desperate Maa Tsuru wondered what was amiss with Fofo. She made to yell an insult. Fofo cut her short. "Mother! Something was coming out of her private part."

Maa Tsuru frowned and then smiled. "Go and call her for me. Then fetch some water for her. She will need it to bath again."

"Yes, mother."

164

"And Fofo . . ."

"Yes, mother."

"Warn her I said she shouldn't soil the whole place with her menstruation."

"Yes, mother."

Fofo spent less than a minute outside and returned. Maa Tsuru landed one look upon her face and knew that something was wrong. Fofo stared at her and said slowly, "The thing coming out of Baby T's *there* is not blood, mother."

Maa Tsuru's brow furrowed. Were her daughters up to some trick? Did they think they would get away with it? She wrenched one *Charlie wotee* from one foot, held it at a ready to strike in the right hand and thumped her way towards the back of the house. She caught sight of Baby T, approached her, laid a good look upon her and knew instantly that all was not well with her. The slipper fell from her hand. She slipped in her foot. "Get up!" she ordered Baby T.

Baby T obliged slowly.

Maa Tsuru instinctively glanced at the back of her dress. Her face clouded with renewed anger. She snatched the Charlie wotee off from beneath her foot again and slapped Baby T with it. Baby T fell back on the concrete floor in a daze. She rubbed her hurting back. The ensuing tears were one of confusion.

"Didn't you say you were not menstruating?" Maa Tsuru screamed, "What is that at the back of your . . ." and blinked, cutting herself short suddenly as the nature of the stain behind Baby T's dress hit her full in the face. She realized her mistake. The stain wasn't blood. She threw down the Charlie wotee, disgusted with herself, and helped Baby T up. Baby T was in obvious pain. Maa Tsuru held her by the waist and made Baby T place her one arm over her shoulder for support because she was limping. They treaded slowly to the house and into the room, ignoring the curious stares. Maa Tsuru laid Baby T down on her mat and made her to spread her legs. She gasped at what she saw. She should as a matter of fact have asked Baby T who did it to her. Somehow she couldn't bring herslf to. She was afraid that the answer would turn out to be the suspicion brewing inside her head. In which case, would the blame not also be equally on her head too? What had she done the first time when he used only his fingers on her?

She began to clean Baby T with a warm towel and wept silently as she did. They were tears for herself more than for Baby T. When did he do it? Where?

Baby T lay there motionless, crying. The pain was distinct in her eyes. The trauma she had suffered had left its prints on her very person and her soul. She was in great physical and an even greater mental pain. If the good Lord gave her long life, it was obvious she was going to require lots of strength and love to rebuild her dignity, her self love and trust.

"Mother!" Baby T called softly and winced.

Fofo walked in with some tablets of paracetamol just then.

"Take the medicine first." Maa Tsuru urged Baby T, seeking to postpone the utterance from Baby T's lips of the name of Kpakpo. "Here!" and held her head up and placed the tablets in Baby T's right palm. Baby T threw them inside her mouth and sipped water from the cup held to her lips. As Maa Tsuru stretched out the empty cup to Fofo to take away, Baby T muttered, "Onko."

It didn't register immediately with Maa Tsuru. She placed Baby T's head gently back on the pillow.

"Mother," Baby T muttered once more, "It was Onko."

16

Maa Tsuru stared long at the thick wad of notes in her hand. There was a look of worry and hopelessness in her eyes and another not so easily discernible. Then she rested her gaze upon Onko's face. Onko found it difficult to return the gaze. He turned his head away. Maa Tsuru sighed heavily. Never once in her entire life till then had she held so much money in her hand. Onko read her thoughts. Strike while it's hot, he thought.

"It is not just for the money, Maa Tsuru," he urged her urgently, "Think also of what would happen to Kpakpo. His name will by all means crop up. I will ensure that. He started it all. He should not have touched her in the first place. He should never have played with her with his fingers. What he did made her curious about trying out the real thing. It was she who started pushing herself on me. You can ask the other children who always come to watch television in my room. She was always hopping on my laps and provoking me. I didn't just get up one day to do it with her. She led me on."

Tears welled up in Maa Tsuru's eyes. "She isn't even yet twelve. Did you know that?"

"I'm sorry Maa Tsuru. Really I am. I am very sorry." Onko sounded really repentant. "I can't even understand how the whole thing happened. The more I think about it, the more I am convinced that it was the devil that made me . . ."

"Spare me that Onko!" Maa Tsuru cut him short sharply.

Onko was taken aback by the severity of her tone. "Does that mean you won't take the money?" he frowned. "Look! Even with my fairly successful welding business, this money in your hand would have taken me a long time to make. And let me assure you that it is not my final present to you. I told you that already, or?"

Maa Tsuru looked him directly in the face. She said nothing.

"I will pay for her treatment too!" he went on hurriedly. "Trust me, Maa Tsuru. It is the best way out. Allow me to show you how generous I can be. Just drop the matter. Forget it ever happened and spare us all the trouble."

Maa Tsuru rose abruptly. Onko's face fell. Then the corners of his lips stretched into a smile as Maa Tsuru untied her cover cloth around her waist; placed the wad of notes in one corner of it and proceeded to slowly tie it up. She did not look once in Onko's face. If she had, she would have seen how the initial trace of shame and remorse had completely disappeared from Onko's face.

It had been three weeks since it happened, when Onko asked Baby T into his room to collect money to buy food for both of them. Kind generous Onko. Three weeks since he had unexpectedly locked the door and pushed an unsuspecting and too trusting Baby T onto his bed, pinned her down, forced a handkerchief inside her mouth and torn off her pants. Three times he did it, and left her bleeding on his bed. "Better tell no one!" he warned. I know what your new father Kpakpo did to you. Fofo told it all to me. Your mother loves him. I will tell it all if you tell anyone."

Three weeks! And there he was, calling her, grinning at her, asking her lewdly, "Baby T how are you doing?" And when Baby T ignored him, went on without shame, "Oh why? Don't you want to mind me again?"

Maa Tsuru was folding things on the bed when a distraught Baby T came and reported what just happened.

"Don't mind him." Maa Tsuru told her.

Baby T remained standing there.

"I said don't mind him!" Maa Tsuru shouted at her and folded the cloth in her hand with a highly-strung urgency.

Baby T left the room quietly. The tears welled up involuntarily.

Maa Tsuru finished folding her things in deep thought. The following day, she watched Onko leave the house for his workshop. An hour later, she paid him a surprise visit there.

"I have noticed what is going on, Onko, and I don't like it!" she confronted him in a low voice to avoid attracting the attention of his apprentices.

"What has been going on?" Onko feigned surprise.

"Since Baby T got back on her feet, you have been grinning lewdly and staring at her behind!" she accused him.

Onko wore a serious look and stepped closer to Maa Tsuru. "I love her!" he muttered without pretence.

Maa Tsuru was shocked into dumbness. She left the workshop wordlessly.

By the time Onko returned home from the workshop that evening, Baby T had been sent away.

Maa Tsuru didn't like the name of the middle woman right from the onset. Mama Abidjan? Didn't that make who she was, or what she had been too obvious? But Kpakpo assured her that, yes, even though Mama Abidjan used to work as a prostitute in the Ivory Coast, eventually graduating to become a Madame, she was now a repented retiree who was into recruiting young girls for work in chop bars and households. Mama Abidjan was a relative, he told Maa Tsuru. And because Mama Abidjan knew his relationship to Baby T, she would guarantee find good placement for her. Wasn't Maa Tsuru's immediate concern to get Baby T as far away as possible from Onko? So Mama Abidjan held a conference with Maami Broni, who agreed to take on Baby T. Mama

Abidjan communicated this to Kpakpo who informed Maa Tsuru, who talked to a quite willing but somehow confused Baby T, who subsequently packed her things ready and left with Maami Broni who came and picked her up from the house to her new unknown life.

Several weeks later, Maa Tsuru tried to find out where her daughter had been put to work. She asked Kpakpo.

"I will find out from Mama Abidjan and let you know!" he promised.

Maa Tsuru repeated the question three days later when nothing came from the first one.

"I didn't meet Mama Abidjan." Kpakpo claimed. "I'll try again today."

Maa Tsuru allowed one week to elapse. She didn't press Kpakpo for an answer any longer. She didn't know where Maami Broni lived, but she knew where Mama Abidjan lived. She paid Mama Abidjan a surprise visit one early morning. Mama Abidjan did not take kindly to the unexpected visit.

"Was it me who came to you and forced you to bring your daughter to me?" she yelled at Maa Tsuru and banged the door in her face.

Maa Tsuru banged the door with her fist till Mama Abidjan opened it again.

"If you don't tell me where I can find my daughter, I will go to the police. And this time, I don't care whether Kpakpo becomes embroiled in it or not." Maa Tsuru threatened.

Mama Abidjan didn't take kindly to the threat but she held herself in check. And to get Maa Tsuru off her back, promised to find out where Baby T was and to let her know the following day. The evening of that early morning that Maa Tsuru paid Mama Abidjan the surprise visit, something even more astonishing by Maa Tsuru's standard, occurred; which to her was akin to a miracle. Kpakpo gave her 'chop money' for the very first time. She was truly astounded. "Have you found work?" she asked him.

"Let's just say, sort of." Kpakpo replied evasively.

The following day, Maa Tsuru waited anxiously for Mama Abidjan to bring her the promised news about Baby T's whereabouts. Surprisingly, it was Maami Broni who turned up. And she was all but pleased with Maa Tsuru.

"No thank you!" she refused the seat Maa Tsuru offered.

"No thank you!" she turned down the offer of a cup of water.

Then she told Maa Tsuru to go to her room and look through her window. "You want to know where I put Baby T to work? Her employer is standing behind your window. Take a look."

Maa Tsuru did and shook like a leaf.

"He said to tell you he is keeping an eye on your younger daughter too!" Maami Broni added before Maa Tsuru could recover from the shock of the sight of Poison behind her window. "If you give him any problem again about Baby T, Fofo would not be left alone. Where did you think the envelopes you have been receiving have been coming from?" Maami Broni snorted.

Maa Tsuru frowned; confused. "Envelopes? What envelopes?" she stuttered.

Maami Broni chuckled. "Are you dumb or just playing dumb? Your share of your daughter's earnings, what else? How do you think we ensured you didn't meddle? What did Mama Abidjan tell you? That she was a one woman charitable organization handing out free envelopes?"

Maa Tsuru grew bewildered. Then Maami Broni frowned as the realization dawned on her that Maa Tsuru was speaking the truth.

For Maa Tsuru, pieces of the puzzle all suddenly fell in place. Kpakpo! The miracle of the 'chop money' was really no miracle at all. He found out about her visit to Mama Abidjan.

"You weren't receiving the envelopes?" Maami Broni roared.

Maa Tsuru thought of Poison stationed there behind her window. Kpakpo the smallish deceitful man, but who nevertheless delivered her from the doldrums of her emotional quarantine.

What was she to say? That Kpakpo was apparently intercepting the envelopes and keeping whatever they contained for himself? Wouldn't she be delivering him on a silver platter to Poison?

"I was," she mumbled. "I was receiving the envelopes."

But after all that Maami Broni saw of Maa Tsuru's reactions, it was too little said too late to clear her suspicion. She decided there and then to handle the deliveries of the envelopes herself. Thus it began, that for years, Maami Broni came to symbolize the arrival of an envelope containing money, whenever she showed up in the house. It always brought a smile to Kpakpo's face and a wince to Maa Tsuru's, who nevertheless never turned it down.

Then came that morning!

Maami Broni's presence in the house for once did not translate into an envelope containing money. It was to break the news of the body behind the blue Rasta hairdressing kiosk at Agbogbloshie.

Maa Tsuru never had the opportunity to find out how Kpakpo would have reacted after wearing his usual broad smile for Maami Broni in anticipation of the envelope only to find out that for that day, her presence did not mean money.

It was because Kpakpo was not around. Three days before, he had unceremoniously left Maa Tsuru and their two young sons.

BOOK THREE

17

Kabria had never disputed the adage that all of God's creations have souls. But she had always placed 'creations' in the limited context of man, plants and animals.

The traditional carver knows what he is doing when he does not just get up to cut a tree to work with. He believes in the appropriateness of pacifying the soul of the tree first, to explain to it why he has to end the tree's life by cutting it down.

Certain inexplicable occurrences also sometimes lend weight to the adage. Like the famous stone in the northern town of Damongo which was moved to make way for a new road construction but which kept returning by itself to its original position. Something that compelled the initially skeptical foreign construction company to eventually redesign the route of the road in order to leave the mysterious stone in perfect peace.

But a car?

A car after all is made of steel. Steel that was dug, God knows where, melted, milled, and moulded into a VW Beetle that had passed through God knows how many hands. Where laid its soul?

Kabria felt pretty justified to be upset with Creamy. There was always something about Creamy to be upset with. Today, it was behaving like everything else but a car. It was literally crawling.

"Peeee . . ." a driver hooted from behind her.

"Not today. Please!" Kabria pleaded with her world.

"Peeee . . ." the driver hooted again.

She was negotiating a roundabout.

"Can't you move?" the driver yelled at her.

Kabria took out her frustration on Creamy. After all what soul did it have?

She pressed her foot on the accelerator down to the floor and hit the steering wheel. "Move!" she yelled at Creamy. "Move like a car. You are not a snail. Move!"

Creamy had no soul? Maybe Kabria should have thought again. For, almost immediately, something almost as bizarre as the stone that wouldn't be compelled to move happened. Creamy stopped dead right there in its track. It was in the middle of the round-about. Tears of embarrassment welled up in Kabria's eyes.

"You can't do this to me!" she wailed.

A policeman directing traffic strolled up to her. The expression on his face spoke volumes.

"Problem?" he asked.

He didn't wait for her reply. He moved to the right side of her windscreen and began scrutinizing her insurance and roadworthy stickers.

Kabria flipped. "Don't worse cars ply this road? Are the roads themselves car worthy?"

The policeman smiled. He was a patient officer. "Put everything in order before you go next time to renew your roadworthy, Madam!" he advised calmly.

"Everything is in order!" Kabria snapped. "It is only a small problem with overflow, I think."

"You think?" the policeman smiled. "Then wait a while and restart the engine."

Kabria took the advice in good stride. Minutes later, Creamy responded to life.

"Thank you!" she muttered to the policeman.

He smiled at her and headed back to his former position.

Owing to the delay caused by Creamy's brief 'strike action', Kabria met only Dina in the office, who informed her that she had already dispatched Aggie and Vickie to the mortuary. "Aggie revealed she knew someone there who could have access to Baby T's post mortem results. Any additional information we gather could prove useful. We suspect Poison, but suspicion is not enough to nail him, is it?"

Kabria agreed. "I keep having the feeling we are missing out on something very minuscule."

"Me too." Dina said.

"I should have joined them to the mortuary." Kabria moaned.

"Next time coax Creamy. Don't hit it!" Dina teased.

"I've learnt my lesson." Kabria laughed.

Dina felt silent and pondered. "If only Maa Tsuru would talk to us!" she cried in despair.

An idea hit Kabria. "What if we convince Fofo to accompany us? She won't refuse to let in her own daughter."

Dina beamed. "We'll need to bring in Sylv Po for the media magic touch. We are in this with Harvest FM."

"I agree. But going there with her daughter without prior notice is not the same as showing up with Sylv Po." Kabria countered. "I struck a good cord with Naa Yomo the first time. Maybe I should go and test the waters with her."

Dina consented. "I will also contact Afi's Agency for any useful information they may have for us. Remember what Afi said about the woman she was staying with who tried to sell her to a certain man?"

A renowned pathologist Sylv Po once interviewed on his GMG show disclosed that in the course of his further studies in Europe, the first time he entered the Teaching Hospital's mortuary, he thought he had missed his way. He had grown so accustomed to mortuaries back home that, he expected stained walls, naked corpses lying on slabs, the peculiar scent of death that clung onto a person for days on end, and mortuary attendants who, having decided theirs was no job executed in sobriety, were boozed on duty. An irony for a part of the world where the dead are revered, and the destinies of the living are tied to the apron strings of ancestors. But insanity reigned where mortal remains lay to be drained of frost prior to being showcased at elaborate funeral celebrations.

Aggie and Vickie sat in a room next to the morgue, juggling with the intricacies of death. Aggie's acquaintance, a male nurse, sitting across from them, listened attentively to Aggie as she spelt out their mission and couldn't hide his bemusement.

"You actually came all the way here to find out about what killed that street girl?"

"Yes." Aggie replied.

"Why? Has she turned out to be a relation of the President?"

"No. She is connected to one of our case files. Can we get a copy of the autopsy report?"

"That would be contravening the rules," he said with a smile. "But I can fill you in with the essential points. It's a favour, even though you broke my heart years back and chose to . . ."

"Do we have to go through that now?" Aggie protested feebly.

He laughed. Aggie and Vickie joined in. Then he resumed saying, "Honestly, whoever this dead streetgirl is, must be very lucky to have two fine women like you come here to find out what killed her. God knows how many bodies are cut up each day and whose causes of death show clear signs of murder but which end up gathering dust because no one was interested."

He flipped through Baby T's report. "She died from a fatal head injury. There was bleeding on the left of her brain."

Vickie took notes.

"There were distinct traces of inner hand prints on her right cheek too!" he went on.

"The palm?" Aggie asked.

"Yes. The report indicates that she was dealt some severe slaps. It is suggestive of a male hand."

178

"Why not female?" Vickie asked.

"The report only expressed an opinion on that aspect," he replied. "It's not as definite as establishing what killed her. But the severity of the hand's impact which resulted in those distinct traces on the cheeks was, though not impossible, quite inconsistent with a female hand."

"So what was the conclusion?" Aggie asked.

"The specimen … I mean, the girl, reeled to her left. She could have been pushed. Or maybe it was the impact of the viscious slap. She may have lost balance, or became dazed or something. She went down as a result and hit the head on something which left the gaping wound to her head."

"Which caused her death?"

"Which probably caused her death!" he emphasized. "There is something else. She did not die where she was found."

"How was that established?" Vickie asked.

"The foreign matter in the open head injury," he replied.

Aggie was surprised. "You go through all such trouble even for unidentified bodies dumped at public places?"

"We don't take chances. Today's unidentified dumped body could turn out tomorrow to be a lost member of the first family," he replied. "Many such reports end up gathering dust, but we are still obliged to continue doing our job."

"So was it a murder case?" Aggie asked.

"The report was inconclusive on that."

"There was talk about all hair on her body being shaven off."

"Yes."

"Was it connected to her death?"

"The report did not establish that."

While Aggie and Vickie, at the mortuary, were sorting out the puzzling pieces of Baby T's death, Kabria paid Naa Yomo a brief visit, unleashing a drama the moment her back was turned.

Inside her room, Maa Tsuru's hands trembled so badly that she set her baby down on the floor beside the older one and listened again.

"Open up!" the voice rasped again, followed by a tap on the door with the walking stick.

Now Maa Tsuru was in no doubt about who it was. She grew bewildered. What was so important as to have dragged Naa Yomo up from her seat, all the way across the compound, which for the old lady was plenty work, to Maa Tsuru's door? She opened it a little and spied. It was Naa Yomo all right. Maa Tsuru opened the door wider to let her in. Naa Yomo refused the invitation. She leaned instead on her walking stick and gruntled, "You lock yourself in here and come out only after you have peeped through your key hole and made sure I am not on my stool. Do you think shutting yourself up this way is what will solve your problem? I am returning to my stool. I want to talk to you."

As she ambled back, the children playing in the compound stared in awe at her back. Many of them could not remember when they had ever seen Naa Yomo tread across the compound from her own room to another's door. She always sat there and summoned. And when you did not respond fast enough, she dealt with you. She was known to reproach anyone she felt had to be reproached. Her favourite target group were women staying in the house with men who hadn't married them, and who obviously had no intention of ever marrying them. Maa Tsuru had had her fair share of it.

Naa Yomo simply deemed it her responsibility to check every one because apart from being the oldest member of the household, every living soul there was directly or indirectly related to the one significant common denominator. The great he, who shook hands with Sir Gordon Guggisberg. In the same vein, and just as equally, she also empathized with those in the house who retired to bed each night praying that one day they would be able to move out of the house and offer their children a better life in an improved environment. With her children and grandchildren out of the house, Naa Yomo understood the frustration of the conscientious ones who failed to exert enough positive influence on their children in that milieu. Those who by virtue of their weak pocket power were compelled to continue staying on in the house because it was rent-free. In the midst of it all, she observed with her inquisitive eyes, listened with her alert ears, and lashed out with her never resting tongue. But she always did that seated in front of her room.

Maa Tsuru came out and walked across to Naa Yomo shortly thereafter. They entered the room together and sat on the old lady's bed.

"Tsuru," Naa Yomo began, "I have known you from the moment you were born. Yet today, I did not sit here to shout your name to summon you. I rose from my seat and ambled to your door. I'll tell you why. You have locked yourself up inside your room. You come out only when you have to. This household regards you as a leper. How you and your two little sons survive in there puzzles me. Now I am telling you this: it cannot go on like that. It must stop. Listen. A woman came to see me. Her name is Kabria. She is from the organization that has been caring for Fofo. They want to know the whole true story. She will be back with a man from a radio station who has been working with them. They are people with good sense. That was why she came to see me. They will come with Fofo. I assured them that this time you would open your door to them. Am I clear enough?"

"Yes, Naa Yomo."

"I don't want them to knock more than once."

"No, Naa Yomo."

"Good. I shall be here, as always. And I shall observe and listen."

"Yes, Naa Yomo."

18

Sylv Po arrived at MUTE to pick up Kabria and Fofo, carrying a recorder and a microphone. He was driving a fine metallic blue VW Golf, sleek and fully air-conditioned.

"Wow!" Kabria exclaimed.

Sylv Po smiled. "I heard you drive a VW Beetle yourself."

"Not the sleek new type. The age-old type. Yes. Creamy."

Sylv Po frowned. "Say that again?"

"Creamy. That is the name of my Beetle."

"Your car has a name?" almost roaring into laughter. He checked himself realizing it was no laughing matter with Kabria. At a loss as to how to proceed with a conversation about a VW Beetle nicknamed Creamy, Sylv Po wisely changed the topic.

"I heard the house we are going to is not far from Agbogbloshie?" he asked.

Kabria nodded.

"Can we take a detour through Sodom and Gomorrah? I want to have a feel of the place."

"With the car?" Fofo asked from the back seat with a chuckle. That Sylv Po should even fathom that there was an access route through the enclave sounded preposterous to her.

Sylv Po got the message. "Can we park the car somewhere and walk through the place then?" he suggested.

"Won't we stand out?" Kabria asked. "I hear they are able to make out strangers in their midst on sight and can be very suspicious about visitors and their missions."

Fofo proposed a way out. "Maybe I can use the opportunity to go and look for Odarley. If I am with you and they hear me asking for someone, they will have less cause to be suspicious."

Sylv Po chuckled. "These 'they', who are they? They must be Accra's most mysterious phantoms."

No one responded.

They parked the car and headed toward the enclave through the Konkomba yam market. Sylv Po was surprised by the relative quiet and the, so to say, existing normalcy, considering all that he had heard about the place. "Where are all the much talked about low class prostitutes, and drug traffickers, and the alleged common to see scattered aborted fetuses?" he asked.

Fofo, back in her old territory, swelled with an attitude. Like smoldering fire suddenly fed oxygen, the old spectre came back to life. "Don't turn! Don't look around. They are watching us!" she warned unexpectedly.

Sylv Po became alarmed. "From where?"

"Cool it!" Kabria came in. "Don't attract attention."

They treaded carefully behind Fofo, now their leader, on high alert. They were nervous. It was too quiet. Unnaturally quiet. Where was the much talked about life?"

"Life begins here in the night and ends at dawn!" Fofo began when they reached a more open space with women and children going about their regular daytime business: washing, cooking and playing. Sylv Po and Kabria relaxed a little. "When the rest of Accra is sleeping, that is when Sodom and Gomorrah and its real inhabitants wake up. Now they are asleep. But even when they are asleep, they remain watchful. The women and children you see and think are going about their regular business are all watching."

Sylv Po stopped in his step. "Are you sure we can go through here?" he asked as they passed through a cluster of wooden shacks.

A woman busily washing a huge aluminium cooking pot kept her head so rigidly down it looked suspicious.

"We can pass here but not through there." Fofo indicated with the hand towards where the woman with the head rigidly down was. "I don't know the password to qualify us to pass through there. That place requires one. The woman appears to be washing her pot but her ears are sharp and ready to hear the password. If we don't utter it, by the time we are through the corridor, we would be stopped and interrogated."

"By 'they'?" Sylv Po whispered.

Fofo chuckled. "Yes."

They took the route requiring no password. Crazy colours were splashed on commercial public bathrooms that were scattered all over. There were no public toilets to go with them. The stench from the crudely dug gutters answered the unasked question. Further evidence was provided free of charge a few feet away where a boy of about eight was squatting at the edge of a stagnant pool of greenish algae-infested water and relieving himself with no qualms at all, under the eagle eyes of the passers by.

"Are you sure you will find your friend?" Kabria asked Fofo.

"Maybe." Fofo replied.

"What if Poison sees you?"

"He won't let me see him if he is around. The message would have reached him by now that I am with some people."

They passed by tabletop mini marts, barbering and hairdressing salons, tailors and dressmaking shops. A video centre that, by all indications, specialized in adult films, had proudly proclaimed on a signpost: 'We Show The Best And Leave The Rest'. A metal workshop producing elaborately designed gates, got Sylv Po wondering what customers patronized them, as no abode in the enclave boasted of a walled house requiring any such gate. A commercial ironing shop left Kabria convinced that the rest of Accra probably had a thing or two to learn from Sodom and Gomorrah about innovations and initiatives.

"One can do anything and everything in peace here so long as one follows the rule." Fofo offered without prompting.

"Which is?" Sylv Po prodded.

"Live in peace, trade in peace, steal in peace, deal in peace, sin in peace, by doing nothing to upset them." Fofo recited.

"The 'they'. There we go again." Sylv Po gruntled.

They got to Fofo's former wooden shack. The door was ajar. Fofo entered alone. A girl of about fifteen was asleep on a piece of cloth on the floor. A baby of about six months was scrambling all over her in obvious search for food or attention or both. An unemptied chamberpot stood in one corner. Huge green flies were ravenously picknicking on its contents. Fofo scowled at the sight of it and tapped the sleeping girl on one arm. The girl started from her sleep.

"I am looking for Odarley." Fofo asked her and proceeded to describe her friend.

The girl flung one arm in the air in apparent protest at being so rudely awakened. "She rents here in the night!" she grizzled. "Shouldn't you have known?" And drifted right back to sleep.

Sylv Po was puzzled. "What was she doing there so fast asleep at this time?" he asked Fofo.

"She is a daytime tenant. She works in the night!" Fofo replied.

Maa Tsuru was waiting for them in the doorway. She led them quickly into the room. Before then they had gone over to greet Naa Yomo. She was pleased at what she saw of Fofo. The children playing in the compound stopped and stared. So too did their mothers.

Inside the room, Maa Tsuru made to embrace Fofo. Fofo went rigid. Maa Tsuru's face fell. She withdrew slowly from her daughter. There was pain in her eyes. "Please sit down!" she muttered to Kabria and Sylv Po.

They took the only two available seats. Fofo didn't wait to be offered one. There wasn't any left anyway. She moved towards the bed and sat down carefully on the opposite end, far from where Maa Tsuru sat slumped with her two little sons. Kabria did the introductions.

"Naa Yomo discussed everything with me." Maa Tsuru responded. Then she turned to Fofo and said, "In the presence of these two people who are strangers to me, I am going to open up my heart to you all without any inhibitions. At the end of it, you may find it in your heart to understand some of my behaviour even if maybe, you would have had the strength to do otherwise. Then maybe, you wouldn't freeze so much if I attempt to embrace you."

She proceeded to recount her life from that dawn several years ago when 'British Accra' woke up to the wails and cries of Kwei's mother . . .

An adage goes that the human mind is not like a paw paw fruit, otherwise, it would always be sliced open first to determine the nature of its contents.

Kpakpo gained the chance and made 'fine' use of it by using and abusing Maa Tsuru and her daughters. But like the classic case of: Which came first? The chicken or the egg, Kpakpo would not have gained the opportunity to abuse in the first place, had Maa Tsuru not acted deliberately blind and let him into her life.

"I am a woman and I was lonely." Maa Tsuru opened up. "He gave me the right words. He said, 'I want to retire to bed with you at night and wake up with you in the morning'. It felt good. I had been without a man since Kwei's final disappearance from our lives. No man wanted me. I was a cursed woman. But cursed or not, I was still a woman. I felt like a woman. I needed to be wanted by a man."

Kpakpo's head was of course no paw paw fruit.

"I have lived here all my life with my children." Maa Tsuru went on, her voice beginning to tremble. She swallowed hard and sighed heavily. "Yet, Kpakpo needed only to tell me that he desired to retire to bed with me and wake up with me, and right away . . ." she broke down.

Tears welled up in Fofo's eyes. "He entered mother's life and pushed us all out of it!" she began, " First my two older brothers, then Baby T, then me. My older brothers couldn't stand it. The old bed creaks. The moanings. God!"

The air in the room could best be described as charged. Sylv Po checked his recorder. It was still rolling.

"Why didn't you try to get your older sons to return?" Kabria asked Maa Tsuru.

She didn't respond.

"Yes, mother. Why?" Fofo burst through her tears.

"Didn't you care enough?" Sylv Po asked.

Maa Tsuru's head shot up like a cobra. "Didn't care enough?" she cried calmly. "You sit there and ask me that? What mother wouldn't care? Even Odarley's mother does care for … "

"Please mother!" Fofo shot in, "Don't say what you don't know. Don't talk what you don't understand. Odarley's mother cares? You cared?"

"I know what I am saying." Maa Tsuru kept her cool. "I suppressed my guilt."

Maybe there is something in the old and rather expensive gag that a woman would rather maintain an unworthy man in her life than be seen as a woman with no man in her life.

"Have you received any more envelopes since Baby T's death?" Kabria asked.

Maa Tsuru shook her head.

"Does Onko still live here?" Sylv Po asked.

"He is hardly seen." Maa Tsuru divulged.

"Naa Yomo rained so much insult on him that he resorted to leaving the house early dawn, well before she woke up, and to return late at night, when he was certain she would have retired to bed." Fofo volunteered.

"She knew!" Maa Tsuru said of Naa Yomo, "But she also understood why the matter could not be reported or taken up. That was why she resorted to the insults."

Sylv Po asked if Maa Tsuru had heard from Kpakpo since he left unceremoniously.

She shook her head.

Kabria asked if she was expecting him back.

Maa Tsuru's solemn reply of, "He left some of his things!" made evident a lingering hope harboured by her that Kpakpo would return. It was heartbreaking to see her continued longing for Kpakpo so clearly in her face. "He is their father!" she went on, as though seeking a desperate reason for so glaringly betraying her ongoing desire for Kpakpo. She fixed a sullen look on her two sons.

Fofo was appalled. "So you will do it again, won't you?" she wailed at her mother. "If he returned today you would let him in and probably get yourself pregnant by him again, won't you? Why? Mother, why? What life have you been able to give those of us you already have? Look at the boys here. Look at me. We have no idea where the two older boys are. Are they dead? I often wonder. Are they alive? Are they in prison? Are they killing people to survive? You don't even know. And Baby T? You offered us all generously to the streets, mother. You made the streets claim and own us. These two at your feet are already going hours without food. Only time, and they will also be venturing out onto the streets to fend for themselves. You grew too used to living off the sweat of your children, especially Baby T, whom you . . ."

"Fofo!" Maa Tsuru cut in sharply.

Fofo ignored her mother. "Baby T is gone, mother!" the tears began to flow freely. "You couldn't even mourn her openly. You couldn't bury her decently. You couldn't even talk about her death. What is it you are looking for, mother? Tell me. You said you were going to open up completely to us in a way you had never done before, to enable us maybe understand you. So let me understand you, mother. What is it you want?" and collapsed in more

188

tears into Kabria's arms. Kabria held her close. The tears flowed in torrents. Tears suppressed for too long. Tears that could not be shed out there on the streets where toughness was the prescription for survival and tears were a sign of weakness. Tears held back lest they reveal her fourteen years. She let it all out.

"I think we should check briefly at Onko's workshop on our way back." Sylv Po whispered to Kabria.

She nodded.

Fofo disentangled herself from Kabria's hold, picked an old cloth of her mother's from the bed, blew her nose generously into it, wiped her face and then, smiled unexpectedly at Kabria. It was a smile through pain. It offered hope that the pain could be overcome.

"You know something?" Fofo addressed Kabria, "Sometimes I imagine myself to be outside of my self. I will float out of myself and watch with pity the miserable life led by this young girl called Fofo. Later, when I reunite with myself, the weight of it all hits me once again. Then I'll shake with misery. And when I happen to be alone, cry."

No one spoke.

Fofo went on. "Odarley was always saying that I fantasise too much. Sometimes she wasn't sure which of the stories I told her were real or imagined. When I float out of myself, I watch this poor girl who is I, and I feel great pity for both mother and me. Isn't that funny?"

Maa Tsuru gruntled sourly. Sylv Po and Kabria exchanged looks, both fascinated by the unexpected journey into the mind of Fofo who without doubt, hated her situation with passion. Was this how many of the girls out there on the streets dealt with the harsh reality of their situation? Floating out of themselves?

"Do you still float out of yourself sometimes?" Kabria asked Fofo after a brief while.

Fofo smiled broadly and replied, "Not since I moved into Auntie Dina's home."

19

Something gnawed at Kabria when she started Creamy with Obea, Essie and Ottu in the back. This was later on in the day after her visit with Sylv Po and Fofo to Maa Tsuru. They were on their way home from their school.

Her instincts told her that it wasn't the visit. Nor was it their fleeting call at Onko's workshop on their way from Maa Tsuru, where they had found Onko not present, but learnt during their interreaction with his senior apprentice that the business was collapsing. "Almost all the apprentices have left!" the senior apprentice revealed in despair. "There are no new orders. It's the talk!" he finished off.

"What talk?" Sylv Po asked.

"Oh! You know . . . the rumour . . . that girl with a cursed mother . . . her sister . . ." and pointed at Fofo. "What he allegedly did to her."

The handprint on Fofo's cheeks the day following their first encounter at the market when she found Fofo beaten up also nagged Kabria. The pathologist's report stated similar handprints on Baby T's cheeks. But something else that she couldn't yet pinpoint was the matter here. She stepped on the clutch. Essie called out to a friend standing near the gate and waved at her. The girl transferred her bright blue lunchbox from her right hand to the left and waved back. The colour 'bright blue' whiplashed swiftly through Kabria's mind. Her reaction was instant and spontaneous. She pulled the handbreak and released the gear into free. She left the engine running and did some brief recollections. The culprit was rearing its head slowly. Yes, she did pack two lunches into two separate lunch boxes that morning. Obea had decided she was too old to be trudging a lunch box along to school and old enough to buy her food from the school canteen. So, Kabria recollected, she did as usual pack for Ottu and Essie, both of whom got out of Creamy that morning, as best as she could remember, holding their lunchboxes. So why was Ottu sitting in the car without his lunchbox? She turned round and asked him.

"It is in the classroom." Ottu replied calmly.

As far as he was concerned, all was perfectly splendid with his world.

In Kabria's world however, her head split into two. "You left your lunchbox in the classroom and came to sit in the car?"

"Yes."

"Why?"

"I went to hide in the toilet and forgot about it."

Kabria halted that line of questioning for the sake of her blood pressure and sought an alternative more practical and sensible solution to the problem. "Obea, go with Essie for his lunchbox, will you?"

"No!" Essie howled.

A strange calmness followed an unheard explosion inside Kabria's head. "Why not?" she asked coolly.

"He insulted me!" Essie squealed.

Creamy's engine was still running. Kabria couldn't take the risk of putting it off and restart it. Yet she needn't be reminded by anyone that Ghana was yet to strike oil in its explorations. Debating what to do about Ottu's lunchbox therefore was an economic factor that could affect her economic situation with Adade lending as much support and understanding as the World Bank and IMF lends to the world's developing countries. She got out with Obea to go for the lunchbox and warned Essie and Ottu to better stay inside the car, scorching heat or not.

They found the lunchbox in the classroom. Its handle was broken.

As they approached Creamy, Kabria saw that Essie had ignored her directive and was out and leaning against Creamy. She was gingerly chewing roasted groundnuts.

"She bought it on credit from the groundnut seller over there and said you would pay when you returned, Mum." Ottu volunteered, hoping to gain some favour to lessen his punishment. He knew Kabria would guess correctly that he deliberately left the lunchbox in the classroom because of the broken handle.

Kabria had no energy left for anything else except to get them all, including herself, out of there.

"How much?" she asked the groundnut seller.

"Two hundred cedis."

Kabria fished out the coin from her purse, held it out to the woman and said, "Maame, please, take a good look at her. She is my younger daughter. Have you?"

The groundnut seller laughed.

"If she comes to you ever again for groundnuts on credit, please, you oblige her at your own risk."

The woman laughed again. "They are all like that," she said.

Kabria smiled. They all got back into Creamy.

"Mum!" Ottu called when they set off.

Kabria ignored him.

He went on anyway. "When you are buying my new lunchbox, please, get me one like . . ."

"Ottu!" Kabria howled.

"Yes, Mum."

"Shut up!"

Kabria went straight to the kitchen without changing when they got home. Abena was late with the garden eggs stew. Her Madam had sent her to the market yet again, she explained, which ate into her closing time. Kabria made a mental note, yet again, to have a word with the Madam.

"Tell Obea to hurry up with her homework and come and assist us here!" she told Abena. "Then get me the cellotape after dinner. Ottu will send the lunchbox to school for another week. I'll mend the handle. That should get him to later handle the new one with greater care."

Kabria stirred the palmoil gravy and lowered the fire. Abena returned to the kitchen and brought out the grinding dish. She removed the boiled garden eggs from the fire. Kabria waited for Obea to join them in the kitchen. After a while, she called Obea to hurry up and come and help. Obea didn't respond.

"Obea!" she called again.

No response.

Kabria placed down the ladle and thumped her way to their room. Obea was idling in front of the mirror. That enraged Kabria all the more. She faced Obea and grabbed her by the ear. Obea winced and squealed. Kabria placed her lips to Obea's ear and shouted, "I said we need some help in the kitchen. Come and peel the . . ."

"Ouch! Mum, ouch!" Obea cringed, wondering why Kabria cut herself short so abruptly.

Kabria released Obea's ear absentmindedly and stared thoughtfully into space.

"Mum, is something wrong?" Obea asked, concerned.

"Go and get me Auntie Dina on the telephone. Hurry!" Kabria responded.

She proceeded to the kitchen while Obea made the call.

"Mum, I have her!" Obea called out.

Kabria told Abena as she rushed to the telephone, "Tell me when you have finished grinding the garden eggs."

She took the receiver from Obea. "Dina, listen to this. Don't interrupt me. Is Fofo there with you? . . . Good! The handprints on both Fofo and Baby T's face they were on their right cheeks, no? . . . Good! . . . Now listen. Call Fofo, . . . yes, let her come and stand before you . . . Are you facing each other? . . . Now, imitate a slap . . . No! No! Don't slap her. Gosh! Dina! Just imitate . . . You have? . . . Now let me task your imagination. Take it that you did actually slap Fofo. Take it that you were so viscious it left your palm prints on her cheek. Which cheek would the palm prints be on? . . . Correct! The left cheek. So do you get where I am heading? . . . You don't? . . . Get this! You naturally landed your right palm on her left cheek. No? . . . You still don't get it? . . . Oh Dina! See! You struck out with your right hand to her left cheek, didn't you?" . . . Good! Now ask Fofo if Poison is left-handed . . . Bingo!"

20

The fast mail service man knocked on MUTE's front door with a smile, announced the mail with a smile, handed out the messenger's receipt book to be signed by Dina with a smile, placed the parcel in Dina's hands with a smile, and turned and walked away to his motorbike with a smile. He had been taught to carry out his duties with a smile. And his smile was infectious. So Dina also read the sender's name with a smile, even though it read rather curiously, 'Abraham Lincoln'. With the contents described rather oddly as 'Sample Cotton (for experiment)'.

"Come and see a strange parcel we have received!" Dina called out to the others.

"I hope it's a pleasant surprise." Vickie remarked.

"I'm sure it will be. People are probably beginning to appreciate what we are doing." Kabria added, filled with great hope.

After all it wasn't always that a group of four women took it upon themselves to crack a street life case and attempt to close in on the chief suspect. It was two days after Kabria had established the left-handed theory. Two days during which Sylv Po had wasted no time with it. The very following morning after Kabria's 'discovery a la Obea' he presented the hypothesis to listeners on the GMG show thus: "The case of the young girl whose body was found behind a rasta hairdressing kiosk salon at Agbogbloshie about three weeks ago, appeared initially to be heading into oblivion, just like many other low profile crime cases involving victims of low social standing. But a chain of uncommon events which was probably brought on by fate more than anything else, changed the course of things and resulted in a bond that was further strengthened with MUTE's curiosity about the mystery of the body behind the kiosk. A body; a streetgirl; an organization. A trinity as simple yet complex as God, the Father, the Son and the Holy Ghost are perfect. Last night I received a very useful call. I am going to let an important cat out of the bag to let the culprit behind the crime know that we are close on his heels. We are putting so much together that when we present it for prosecution, the culprit will not be able to extricate himself. We are on the heels of a left-handed person. Most likely, a left-handed man. So anyone out there with any information should please get in touch with us. Thank you!"

'Abraham Lincoln? Sample Cotton? When two days before, Kabria had established the left-handed theory and the day before, Sylv Po had made his hypothetical presentation?'

Something should have clicked in Dina's or any of the others' head.

Dina proceeded to unwrap the parcel. She was later to wonder what went wrong with her nose that moment, considering she was suffering from no cold or catarrh, because it was Kabria, standing next to her on her right, who first twitched her nose, followed by Vickie who sniffed in her immediate surrounding air with great suspicion. As for Aggie, she twitched, sniffed, twitched again, then held the nose just when Dina shrieked and darted off to the toilet where she dropped the offending parcel right into the Water Closet where literally, it rightly belonged.

For the next thirty minutes, the three watched in anguish Dina go through a 'Lady Macbeth-like' act, wringing her hands in an unending effort as though to rid it of the 'blood'. First she washed her hands with perfumed soap, then decided that the perfume in the soap might conceal the 'scent' without necessarily clearing it off her hands, so re-washed it with an odorless washing soap. Still not satisfied, she rinsed the hands twice in a disinfectant solution, decided the scent of the disinfectant reminded her of the 'scent' of the parcel, so poured ample WC cleaning gel into her palms and resumed the wringling act for another five to ten minutes. She rinsed that away and washed the hands a final time with the perfumed soap again. Then she called Sylv Po.

"We just received a shit parcel!" she told him.

"We just received an odd anonymous call!" he told her.

The caller to Harvest FM at around the same time that MUTE's parcel was being delivered, didn't ask for Sylv Po or anyone in particular. She also didn't allow for time. She launched straight into business as soon as Sylv Po's producer, who received the call, said "Hello."

The information she gave was old news. She knew the dead girl, she claimed. The caller to the station day's ago who alleged that the dead girl was a *kayayoo,* called Fati, was a liar. The dead girl was certainly Baby T, she added.

Sylv Po's producer could have yawned. "Do you know the killer?" he asked.

"The left-handed man, you are on the right track!" the caller replied.

This time the producer actually feigned a yawn to convey his mood to the caller. "Why should we believe you?" he asked.

"I was the one who slaughtered a white fowl at where Baby T was found!" she replied.

That snapped Sylv Po's producer out of his boredom. "Why?" he asked the caller.

"To appease her spirit!" she replied calmly.

Then she replaced the receiver gently.

21

It cuts across genders, but it seems to be more prevalent with young males. Maybe it has to do with the faceless formless masculine thing, whatever that 'thing' is. What appears to be the case, though, is that it is more difficult to break the 'streetness' in boys from the streets than in girls. Abused young males, in particular, are also more prone to becoming abusers themselves.

Poison ran from home at the age of eight to hit the streets. Home was a two by four room in a compound house in an Accra inner city, which he shared with his mother and stepfather and five siblings. He was an extremely shy boy; very soft spoken and covered from head to toe in scars gained from several years of lashes with a man's leather belt at the stepfather's hands. The stepfather used to boast that he delighted in whipping Poison for the joy of it. His mother was always compelled to look on helplessly. The one time she attempted to intervene, the belt was turned on her.

Poison landed in bad company on the streets the moment he landed there. Within days, he had mastered in car tape-deck thefts. The more he stole, and got away with, the more confident he became. And the more confident he grew, the more he felt in control of the streets. But as he controlled the streets, or felt he was controlling them, the more the streets also controlled him. After three years stealing car tape-decks, Poison became bored with it. He desired change. In his quest for that change, he ended up perching with a girl six years his senior. Her room was in an inner city brothel situated inconspicuously in the midst of a cluster of low, run down houses. He became her messenger and ran errands for her 'supervisor' too.

An errand for the supervisor often involved going to one of his 'girls' with a load of warnings and threats, to instill fear in the girl, and get her to part willingly and immediately with the supervisor's share of her previous night's earnings.

An errand for the girl often involved tucking away a portion of her earnings, which she did not disclose to the supervisor, somewhere safe, and sending it later to a relation who regularly banked the money for her. By age fifteen, Poison had mastered the intricacies of pimping enough to have a go at it on his own. He had no problem at all forming his gang. He had made a mark and a name on the streets already. Next was the fight for control and a share of the streets. Then he embarked on an aggressive recruitment of girls to own.

One of his first groups of girls provoked him shortly after he put them to work, by refusing to service a client according to his desire. Poison had her brought into his room. He locked the door, stripped her naked, lashed her mercilessly with a men's leather belt; then raped her. The other girls never dared to provoke him.

Poison, in addition to this single act of extreme brutality, gained more fame in his world with his loud-mouthed acknowledgement that yes, his life was not on the right track and hell be his witness, but he would ensure that the life of others never landed on the right path either.

He was seated on a bench on the veranda of his abode and surrounded by members of his gang when Kabria and Sylv Po were brought to him. The gang member to his immediate right had been promoted to 'lieutenant' just the previous day. He had earned this promotion through pleasing Poison enormously when he had successfully ensured the delivery of his own beautifully parcelled solid waste material, passed from his own bowels, to MUTE. To Poison, MUTE was the cause of most of his headaches about the increasing public interest in Baby T's death. They brought it to the attention of the media through Sylv Po, and the shit parcel was a message to them not to meddle in other people's business.

His tough build was menacing and his two facial scars, scary. One run sharp and diagonal through his left eyebrow, disrupting the hair flow. The other was vertical, slanted and long. It could be mistaken for a tribal mark except that on second look, one noticed that it began not from under the corner of the eye adjacent to the beginning of the nose ridge but somewhere beneath the middle of the eye, right down to below the jaw line. He exuded jungle power and smiled like the confident controller of the streets that he was. Kabria shuddered at the intermittent stares he fixed on her. The right corner of his lips extended into a wry smile at one point, indicating he had noticed Kabria's discomfort and was enjoying watching her squirm. Sylv Po did most of the talking, and while he talked, Poison never interrupted him once. Finally, when he did speak, it was to say simply, "I did not kill Baby T. I left her alive!"

The meeting with Poison was made possible through a little coercion, a touch of blackmail, and a bit of deceit.

Dina contacted the agency that had hired out Afi to her and inquired about the woman from whom they 'saved' Afi before she could be sold into prostitution. Naturally, the Agency was reluctant to co-operate. It wouldn't be good for their business if it should emerge that they went about sharing information they were privy to with other bodies and organizations. Sylv Po was knowledgeable about the modus operandi of such Agencies. Even though their business was legitimate, and they sometimes advertised their services in the media, they mostly recruited by word of mouth. They dealt mostly with girls because girls were mostly preferred when it came to placements into households. All sorts

of girls usually reported to them to seek household jobs, like teenage school dropouts, who having had a tough go at life, had realized that free life was really not free. Precisely why the Agency
needed their 'sources' to check and verify the backgrounds of
such girls. Another instance was a girl brought in from the village,
like Afi was, under the pretext of coming to serve and receive an
apprenticeship training of a sort in return, and who realizes too
late that she was about to be sold into prostitution. Such a girl,
who hears by word of mouth about the Agency, as Afi did, and
goes to them, was likely to see herself as having been 'saved' by
the Agency and be eternally grateful to them and more subservi-
ent to the household she is sent to serve. The agency preferred
such girls. Their income after all, depended on the reliability of
the girls to the household they served, because part of what the
girls were paid went to the Agency as their commission. The more
reliable, dutiful, and trouble-free a girl hired out by the Agency
was to the household, the better for the Agency's overall reputation. And the higher their reputation, the more daring they could
be in their price quotations. Therefore, as regards their preferred
girls, the Agency sometimes did not wait for a distressed girl to
decide by herself to come to them and be 'saved'. But soon as
their sources smelt distress, they moved in to convince the girl to
go to the Agency, which was what had happened in Afi's case. It
therefore stood to reason that the Agency and their 'sources' knew
the woman who wanted to sell Afi to the streetlord. The woman
therefore must have been in connivance with the streetlord. And
Accra's streetlords knew each other. They were not necessarily
friends, but they took cognizance of each other in order to, as
much as possible, avoid stepping on one another's toes. The
Agency's problem, though, was that it would undermine the confidence of their 'sources' should they co-operate with MUTE and
Harvest FM. At this point, therefore, Sylv Po subtly released a
hint into the grapewine. Harvest FM was considering doing a series on the Agency. One focus of attention would be that, though,

they help place girls in household jobs, sometimes they inadvertently shield and protect law breakers like the woman who nearly sold Afi into prostitution. The Agency promptly did a U-turn and agreed to co-operate. They put their 'sources' to work. A message reached Poison that a 'consignment' was being expected. In Poison's world, it meant fresh young girls recruited from poor villages under a similar pretext as Afi had suffered. The woman bringing the consignment, Poison was told, wanted to meet him together with her partner. At the scheduled meeting, Kabria showed up with Sylv Po. They did not hide their true identity and Poison was truly awed by their interest in Baby T.

"That girl?" he howled initially; then displayed an unwillingness to co-operate with them.

Sylv Po played his trumpcard. Did Poison know that the media could undo him by mounting a pressure campaign to compel the law to take its due course?

Poison smiled bitterly. "I'm listening!" he muttered.

Sylv Po cleared his throat. "If you truly did not kill Baby T, as you are claiming, then it would be in your own interest to work with us to fish out who did. Because really, everything points to you and everyone has already concluded that you are the killer. You went and warned Maa Tsuru. Many would testify to it that they saw you, and even Maa Tsuru would be compelled to, under court order. You attacked Fofo. Odarley and the others would also testify to that, if not willingly, then under court order. And as you must have heard on my programme, which prompted you to send that 'fine' parcel to MUTE, it has been established that a left handed person beat up both Fofo and Baby T prior to her death. See my point?"

Poison mellowed. "I did beat the girl up, but I did not kill her!" he repeated. "Why would I kill a girl who was making lots of money for me? Maami Broni would bear me out. You can talk to her if you like. I did beat her up but I left her crying, not dead. She wouldn't be crying if she was dead, would she?"

"Where can we find Maami Broni?" Sylv Po asked.

Poison asked his newly promoted lieutenant to describe the direction to her place.

Sylv Po conferred briefly with Kabria, then excused himself and called Dina on his cell phone.

Poison grew nervous watching all this. "Look!' he boomed as soon as Sylv Po rejoined them. "I am a businessman. You may not like what I do but that is what I do. It is my business. Why would I so foolishly and carelessly jeopardize it by killing one of my girls?"

Kabria, who had all this while been the silent observer, stared Poison direct in the face for the first time. She believed him. It wasn't common sense. It was instinct.

Sylv Po asked Poison if he was aware of the three anonymous calls to Harvest FM.

Poison didn't respond.

"The first two callers claimed that the dead girl was a Fati who deserved to die because she jilted her old husband." Sylv Po went on. "The second caller refuted the first caller's claim and insisted the dead girl was Baby T. Both were anonymous. Do you know anything about it?"

Poison glared at Sylv Po and rose abruptly, catching even his gang members off guard. Kabria shook visibly. Sylv Po stood his ground and stared Poison right back in the eyes. The fleeting tension doubled the weight of the surrounding air. Then suddenly, Poison chuckled and roared into laughter. The gang joined in. Laughter galore.

Without warning, Poison slumped back into his seat and wore a dead serious look. "I had the first two calls made to your station!" he told Sylv Po. "As I said, I am a businessman. It was nothing more than a business ploy. People knew Baby T was one of my girls. I had already silenced her mother. But what about the others? I didn't want any unnecessary disturbances."

"You didn't say why you had the calls made. And what unnecessary disturbances were you trying to avoid?" Sylv Po pressed on.

Poison was amused. "You talk a lot on the radio like you are a smart guy but you are not smart at all, are you?" he taunted Sylv Po.

Sylv Po kept his cool.

"Isn't it obvious why I had the calls made?" he sneered.

"No. Tell me. I am not smart at all. You just said it yourself, no?" Sylv Po played crafty.

Poison chuckled. "If I made people believe that the dead girl was someone called Fati, then it meant that Baby T was not necessarily dead, no?" Poison reasoned vainly. "And if Baby T was not dead, then why would anyone become curious about what happened to her? Or indeed even think that something had happened to her?"

22

"So who killed her? Who killed Baby T? And why?" Dina posed.

No one had an answer.

"You said you believed him?" she asked Kabria.

Kabria winced. "It is not really about what I believe, is it?" cautious about putting her head on the block for Poison. "It's the instinct thing. I was dead scared sitting there with him and his gang. I was most uncomfortable. Every part of me yelled 'guilty' at him. Except my instincts."

It was a meeting of MUTE's four with Fofo, to decide on her rehabilitation, which was preceded with events of the previous day. Dina, who also went looking for Maami Broni following Sylv Po's call to her, found her absent and learnt from a co-tenant who thereafter disappeared into her room that, "Nowadays Maami Broni doesn't even sleep here, oh! She is afraid of her room and the man with the facial scars."

It was an inner city compound house comprising six rooms and operating as an informal brothel. Maami Broni's room was second from the gate.

"So are we back to square one?" Aggie asked dully. "Poison wants a confirmation of his innocence sought from Maami Broni who has also disappeared because she fears Poison? What is happening?"

Dina directed that they leave that to hang and go on to tackle Fofo's rehabilitation issue. "I contacted some organizations with training facilities who are willing to take you on, Fofo. So now it is up to you."

Fofo's face clouded. "I don't have money!" she wailed.

"It is not about money. We will seek support for you." Dina explained. "It is about whether you are willing and prepared for change. It is the first condition towards rehabilitation. You must confirm your desire for the change first, before we can even proceed with this discussion. Do you really want to leave the streets? Have you thought seriously about it?"

"What are the implications?" Fofo asked hesitantly.

"The implications? The first and obvious one would be a level of disassociation from your old friends."

"Odarley too?"

"Probably. But maybe after you have settled into your new life, you can convince her to also leave the streets." Dina replied.

"Will I have to leave your house if I agree to go to that organization?"

"Yes."

Fofo frowned. That obviously didn't please her.

Dina seeing that, added quickly, "But if you don't go into rehabilitation, you will have to leave anyway, because then on what grounds are we keeping you? But if you go into rehabilitation, you will always be welcome to visit. The four of us will also be visiting you regularly."

Fofo digested that and liked it. "Then I'll go!" she declared.

"Wonderful!" Dina exclaimed. "Let's proceed then." And ruffled through the sheets of paper in her hand. "The points are here!" she went on. "First is your interest. What you want to do. What do you want to do? Do you wish to return to school?"

"No! I can't go to school."

"You can't or you don't want to?" Dina asked.

"I don't like it. I don't want to."

"How about something informal?"

"Informal?"

"Yes. You can learn a trade if that is what you want. Then alongside learning the trade, you improve on your basic reading and arithmetic. It will help you in your future trade."

Fofo was not enthused.

"We can't force you to do it, but give it some thought, will you?" Kabria urged her.

Fofo nodded.

Dina moved onto the next point. "The organization offer dressmaking, hairdressing, catering and beadsmaking. Which one do you like?

Fofo shrugged.

"The decision must be yours." Kabria told her. "You must make the choice."

Fofo pondered. "I like catering!" she declared.

Dina took note. "The next point is your background survey," she stated.

"Isn't the organization supposed to carry that out themselves?" Vickie asked.

"If it hasn't been done already, yes. But if we can present them with the information when she reports to them, then all the better. Especially considering the extent of our involvement with her and her family." Dina replied.

"What kind of information are they looking for?" Aggie asked.

"The usual. Her family. Why and how she got caught up in life on the streets. Her chances of returning into her family fold. Things like that."

"Do you think you can return to live with your mother one day?" Kabria asked Fofo.

"Never!" Fofo spat.

Kabria smiled. "Never say never, Fofo."

Dina decided they hold on with the determination of that till later. She moved to the next point. "Fofo, you are expected to go for a comprehensive check-up at the Korle-Bu Hospital. They want to know if you have . . ."

"AIDS?" Fofo cut in.

"It isn't just AIDS." Dina sought to explain.

"I don't have AIDS!" Fofo shrieked hysterically.

Kabria tried to calm her down. "Fofo, listen. There are other sexually transmitted diseases. It isn't only AIDS. There is gonorrhea, syphilis, herpes … "

"But why should I do test?" Fofo shrieked on.

"Because they need to know, so that what is curable, can be dealt with." Kabria explained.

"And the incurable?" Fofo snapped.

"You will be counselled on how best to go on living with that situation. You were sexually active out there on the streets. No?"

Fofo stared into space.

"Look," Kabria held her by the shoulders, "our duty here is not to judge or condemn you for your past sexual behaviour. But we must face reality and deal with it because you did indulge in some careless and unwise sex. We can't wish it away and pretend it didn't happen. Do you understand?"

Fofo mumbled inaudibly.

"Look!" Kabria went on. "It can turn out that you have none of the STD's I mentioned."

"What if I do?" Fofo muttered.

Kabria held her close. "If it is gonorrhea or syphilis, it can be cured."

"And AIDS?"

"Let's deal with it when we come to it."

Dina allowed a brief period for all to regain their composure, and turned their attention back to her sheet. "So now shall we … "

'Ko-ko-ko!' a knock on the door cut her short. It was the office day watchman. "There is a girl under the tree asking for Fofo." He told Dina.

"Why didn't you bring her in?" Dina reproached.

"I tried to but she refused."

Dina called Fofo and went out together with her to meet whoever the girl was. The others came to stand on the veranda to watch.

Fofo recognized her friend from a distance and broke into a run. Odarley run to meet her halfway. They embraced; sized each other up, embraced again, each asking the other how she was doing.

"Won't you invite her inside?" Dina prodded Fofo.

Odarley shook her head vehemently.

"They are nice people, Odarley!" Fofo urged her friend.

Odarley shook her head more vehemently. "I am not staying long. Maybe another time."

Fofo didn't press her any further. "How did you find here?" she asked Odarley.

"Naa Yomo. She sent me. She made one of her sons who was visiting, the one who works with a Bank in Sunyani, drop me at the junction. I continued to here on foot. They gave me money for my transport back. I would have found this place easily anyway. Everybody is talking about you and this organization."

"Are you sure you don't want to come inside?" Dina asked Odarley.

Odarley shook her head.

Dina excused herself and turned back to the office.

Odarley held Fofo by one hand and put her lips to Fofo's ear. "Something happened. Onko is dead."

Fofo's eyes widened.

"God punished him at last!" Odarley whispered on.

"Because he died?"

"Because of the manner in which he died." Odarley went on. "He killed himself. Suicide. He hanged himself on a tree."

It happened not far from his workshop and he was in a pair of light blue shorts, the colour of the skies. "Was he entreating God for a last minute reconciliation?" someone asked.

He left no note.

The police came for his body; then visited his workshop. Then they went and informed Naa Yomo about it, she being the oldest member of the household.

Onko's senior apprentice did not tell everything he knew to the police. He was skeptical about what use they would put it to. But he could not afford to hide that kind of information from Naa Yomo, just in case some rituals needed to be performed to put Onko's spirit to rest. The spirit is said to always hover aimlessly and restlessly in deaths from suicide. God is said to always categorically ban such spirits from entering His kingdom. When they headed down below too, the devil is said to often bluff them well well, because had they not been rejected up there, would they have come to him? Huge bribes are often said to be demanded of them. And since many in such deaths are often buried with no ornaments, many such spirits often find it impossible to pay the bribe. They are therefore refused entry there too, which leaves them with no alternative but to hover and disturb the living with their unwelcome presence on earth.

"We lost a lot of business after the case with Baby T!" the senior apprentice told Naa Yomo.

Naa Yomo showed no pity even to a man now turned ghost. She did not mince her words. "He deserved it!" she scoffed. "There are many equally efficient welders around. Why should they patronize one who has brought such ill-luck upon his head? He would have been transferring particles of his ill-luck to them through handling their jobs. I hope he had the good sense to pray for forgiveness before his final breath left him."

"I hope so too!" the senior apprentice muttered. "It was God he needed, not the jujuman he consulted."

"He consulted a jujuman on whether he should hang himself or not?" Naa Yomo spat.

"Oh, Naa Yomo. No! He sought the jujuman's services to turn round the misfortune of his business."

"Then he was more unwise than I even thought. He should have solicited the jujuman's help to seek the forgiveness of the gods. Things would have turned round by themselves after that."

It was information, Naa Yomo also agreed, that the police would most likely do nothing with. And really, what should they do? Find out if the jujuman had prescribed his suicide? But Naa Yomo felt that something in the revelations could be of some interest to MUTE and Harvest FM. That was why she sent Odarley to Fofo.

Sylv Po was done with that morning's GMG show but was on the phone with a woman who had called earlier into the programme during the phone-in session and requested to talk with Sylv Po off air after the show. She wanted to present a situation that was similar to that of Fofo's, she claimed; and to pose a question.

"Take it that I am the oldest of five children," she began. "Our father is jobless, yet whatever little money comes his way, he wastes on booze. He beats us up indiscriminately, our mother included. We are all completely intimidated by him. Like my two siblings after me, who are also of school going age, I don't go to school. There is no money. We three older ones go out onto the streets everyday to make money for our upkeep. Our two younger siblings often go hungry. What money we make on the streets, and give to our mother to run the house, our father bullies out of her to waste on booze. Yet, in spite of all this, mother is carrying yet another child. And I am certain it is not the last child she will be carrying. I want to know if I can apply any existing law to legally prevent our parents from having any more children after the one presently carried is born."

Sylv Po found out that it was a real situation. The woman on the line was asking it on behalf of the 'oldest child' who was her househelp. He promised to delve into the situation and tackle it on one of his coming shows. "It should be interesting to hear what bodies like the National Commission on Children, the Commission on Human Rights and Administrative Justice, FIDA, the

National Council on Women and Development and the Attorney General and Minister of Justice would have to say on that!' he responded.

His producer signaled him at this juncture that Dina had sent Vickie over with a message. Sylv Po listened intently to what Vickie had to say and said, "Let me get my things. We will pass the workshop and pick up the senior apprentice."

23

There is something about a jujuman that makes it extremely difficult for people who, without malice, desire to seek an understanding of the rationale behind having to worship without question, the only begotten Son of God who is not of their skin colour. For a country, a continent, a race, still reeling under the effects of the blatant rape of her dignity, the daytime robbery of her resources and the callous exploitation of his very being by the very other race who came holding the Bible in one hand and the gun in the other, one reality remains befuddling and confusing. Why did God the Father choose to let His Son come not in their skin colour but that of the other race? What subtle message lay beneath that, if any?

One such befuddled and confused mind, while not in any way questioning the integrity of the Creator, still couldn't help wondering aloud once, why God, knowing the limitations of man, and the often times that 'doubting Thomas' mind of his, didn't just 'cut the matter short' by simply letting His Son be manifested as three colour skins in one. A Blackman, a Whiteman, a Yellowman?

Those of the race that was raped, robbed and exploited, who in spite of it, have been won over to the side of the religion brought in by the race who did the raping and robbing and exploiting, in order not to get too rational about the race thing, have sensibly and safely adopted the cardinal rule of: 'Do not think. Do not ask questions. Just believe and worship. Period!' and made it their most comforting pillow. Indeed, to be rational would imply seeking alternatives. And therein comes the jujuman.

The jujuman is many times, unclear, confusing and not the regular guy's most attractive alternative.

Vickie for instance, shuddered at the sight of the strange animal skulls and bones covered in blood. And Sylv Po neither understood nor liked one bit, the idea of being commanded to walk backwards after he grinned at a rather funny looking wooden statue, which in fact, appeared to be grinning at him in the first place.

"What did I do wrong?" he wanted to ask the jujuman. "The wooden guy stood there grinning at me anyway and I am your regular guy who deemed it rude not to reciprocate."

But that could have worsened his case and culminated in an order to him to vamoose from the shrine. And he couldn't afford that. They needed audience with the jujuman. They needed to find out about Onko's consultative visit prior to his death. Not to mention that, their fact finding call on the jujuman had already cost them the equivalent of two bottles of schnapps and two fowls, in cash, converted at the jujuman's so to say, 'rate of exchange' and his special mode of estimated MUTE and Harvest FM's bill.

The jujuman did not, even if for the sake of sheer politeness, attempt to hide that yes, he knew clip and clear the reasons for Onko's business woes. So wouldn't it have been better and more prudent for him to have advised Onko to go and appease Baby T's soul inside her violated body and to seek the forgiveness of the gods? Couldn't he have advised Onko to right the wrong he had done, in the physical too? Shouldn't he have asked Onko to seek Baby T's forgiveness and help somehow his own self to deal with the root of his unhealthy desire? Cases of defilement by family members can continue, as happen in many cases, to be hushed in order to, as the popular saying goes, protect the family's name and dignity. Money can go on changing hands to silence the young, often poor victim and their families. What cannot be silenced and hushed and controlled, are people's attitudes and reactions to the defiler. In seeking the jujuman's intervention to revamp his business, Onko sought an impracticable solution to a practicable problem. The crafty jujuman knew and understood that line of the game. He gave Onko what Onko rather unreasonably, but sadly, truly wanted, after listening carefully to Onko's narration of what Onko claimed he suspected to be the cause of his business woes. Which was that the girl he defiled, was the daughter of a cursed woman. The jujuman, the moment he became privy to this information, wasted no time at all in prescribing the requirements to diffuse what he immediately diagnosed to be a mix up of Onko's good blood with that of Baby T's polluted and cursed blood. Then he gave Onko his list. It included four bottles of schnapps, two of which had to be Heinekenns schnapps, made in Holland. Two of the deities to be consulted, he explained, had developed the singular taste for that particular brand of foreign schnapps. The other items on the list were six yards of pure white calico, an amount of cash, a piece of Baby T's pubic hair and a pure white home bred fowl fathered by a pure black home bred cock. After all, who had ever seen a half-caste fowl?

Jujumen are very crafty people. When they know very well they can't solve a particular problem, they simply slip into their list of demands, one demand almost impossible to obtain, not even with their intervention, and which they will almost certainly tell you that that was one item the gods will be offended to have converted to cash. You have to get it pronto in its original form! Period!

The jujuman's such impossible item was Baby T's pubic hair. But jujumen being men after all, were also prone to making mistakes. The jujuman underestimated Onko's determination and miscalculated. He thought that Onko's biggest headache would be Baby T's pubic hair. It wasn't. It was the fowl that should be a half-caste that however, must not be a half-caste according to the demands of the gods. In this day and age of poultry farms where the white fowls are mostly succulently tender broilers fed poultry products right from when they were yolks inside eggs inside 'Mama's belly, where was he to go get this pure white home bred fowl? When did he become the 'fowl-spy' playing James Bond? Agent 00F with speciality: fowls perhaps? How was he to establish which cock had done what with which hen to produce what fowl?

"Did he get one?" Sylv Po asked the jujuman.

The jujuman smiled pompously. "He did with my help."

Sylv Po's curiousity soared ninety degrees. "How?' he asked.

"You see," the jujuman squinted one eye, "In this present world of ours, people think only of the physical and leave the spiritual. It permeates every aspect of our lives including our relation with the world of fowls."

"The world of fowls?"

"Yes. See! Tell me, when you come across a fowl, what goes through your mind? Don't ponder over it. Be forthright. Instinctive. Spontaneous. Look at me. I am a fowl. You are looking at me. I who is a fowl. What flashed through your mind?"

Sylv Po smiled. "Fried or grilled!"

The jujuman glared at him. Sylv Po's smile disappeared pronto. The jujuman chuckled. "See? That is where you and me differ. You saw food on the table, I saw sacrifice. I saw the gods. Spirituality. If you were a fowl and I was looking at you, I would say to myself: Is this fowl fit for a sacrifice onto the gods? That was why I encouraged my nephew to go into the business of rearing special fowls for sacrificial purposes. He rears all kinds. Black fowls fathered by white cocks. Fowls hatched from eggs laid at exactly 12 o'clock midnight. And of course pure white fowls fathered by pure black cocks."

"And your nephew runs this poultry . . . sorry . . . special farm?"

"Exactly. Because I saw beyond the physical. I thought of the spiritual."

"Then I take it that when people come to consult you and you require one such special fowl, you simply refer the person to your nephew."

"Yes."

"And Onko required such a special fowl no doubt, to revamp his business."

"Yes. And that woman also."

"What woman?"

"The fat red woman. She required a fowl. To appease the girl's spirit which was haunting her."

"Maami Broni was being haunted by Baby T's spirit? Did she say why?"

"Yes. That the girl was living with her at the time of her death."

"That's it?"

"Yes."

"So she too bought the fowl from your nephew and brought it to you?"

"No. She bought it and slaughtered it at where the girl died. Behind a blue Rasta hairdressing kiosk at Agbogbloshie, I heard."

Sylv Po's mind raced. Where would he fit in these new revelations on the GMG show?

"Would you like to visit my nephew's farm sometime? Maybe feature it into one of your programmes at your radio station?"

Sylv Po couldn't help but admire the jujuman's quick business sense. "I will discuss it with my boss!" he promised.

The jujuman smiled. "I am sure you will learn something from him. It is a fine farm. The fowls are expensive. You can understand that, can't you? Considering they are specially reared fowls. But they are worth every cedi. The fat red woman even bought two. Very expensive, but she insisted on buying two even though I prescribed only one for her."

Sylv Po frowned. "Why did she do that?" he asked.

The jujuman shrugged. "Maybe she was hoping for a faster end to the spiritual haunting by the girl with a double sacrifice. I get cases like that."

"Then she must have been in real turmoil." Sylv Po remarked. "She was."

"Two fowls instead of the one prescribed?" Vickie howled on their way from the jujuman.

Sylv Po smiled at her. "Well at least you found your voice back!" he teased.

They were the first words Vickie had uttered since they entered the shrine. "I didn't understand something that he said," she went on. "He seemed to be under the impression that Baby T died at the spot where her body was found. What about the 'she was dumped there' theory?

Sylv Po didn't respond. He had also been thinking about the same thing.

24

It is a formidable task to begin to just try to assign reasons, let alone attempt to comprehend why a middle-aged woman who could be somebody's mother or grandmother, who probably is indeed somebody's mother or grandmother, would allow her conscience to sink so low as to agree to put a girl who could be her daughter or granddaughter, into the trade of prostitution without qualms, and make it her task to train a young girl to become good at trading her body for sex. Maybe Maami Broni would not have accepted Baby T under her wings had she not been told what she was told by Poison as was also told him by Kpakpo and Mama Abidjan.

"She is already giving herself to men freely!" she was told about Baby T. "She even almost enticed her stepfather on one occasion. Poor man. He fought her off like she was the very devil."

It dwindled Maami Broni's guilt to zero. If Baby T liked sex as was being alleged and was already doing it anyway with men old enough to be her father, for free, then why not put her in the business and make it profitable for everyone?

Like all the other middle aged women occupying the six-room compound house brothel, Maami Broni, like Mama Abidjan, was an old 'graduate' of Ivory Coast's red light district. It is no secret that the trade is cruel to age and uncompromising to wrinkles. A middle aged woman could have accumulated all the 'know how' of the trade's tricks and all the acrobatics and styles of the act.

Still a man would go for youth. " 'Body call!' So the middle aged like Maami Broni, on their return from Abidjan in Ivory Coast or Agege in Nigeria, or wherever it was they went to hustle, usually set up camp, hunted for novices and launched their own sort of, 'intermediate technology transfer' programme. Normally, the seasoned middle-aged woman takes on the young girls initially as househelps. While carrying on their normal jobs as househelps, the 'apprenticeship' training is subtly launched. The girl could be washing the dishes somewhere behind the house and the Madam would approach her and say something like, "Mr. K needs a bit of help to relax but I have a severe headache. Can you go into the room and see if you can give him what he wants?"

Backpass!

As the young girl picked up the trade, a form of transition took place. The girl ceases gradually to 'profit' from Madam's male 'backpasss'.

While her mother is stuck up somewhere in their poor village thinking that her daughter who was taken by this 'kind and considerate' relation to the city to help her 'get on in life' was probably at that moment, learning how to join the seams of a *kaba* together, the daughter may indeed be busy building a clientele of her own. Eventually, she begins to make more money than her Madam, as the men prefer her young taut body to that of the older flabby Madam. That is when, if the Madam operates solo and is not attached to any streetlord, trouble could begin to brew for her. The streetlord sometimes arranges for customers, but his foremost task is to ensure the protection of both Madam and the girl. And when he is a good businessman, like Poison was, he ensured that he kept everyone happy, including the girl's mother or parents.

Maami Broni and Poison went back a long time. A good number of girls had passed through her hands under Poison's protection. Many were now on their own. Maami Broni could therefore be said to know her job well. The master carpenter can say of an apprentice, "He was born to be a carpenter." Or, "He can never be a good carpenter however much he tries."

Baby T was sweeping the room when Maami Broni entered and said, "Baby T, Mr. F wants to come in here. Can you pause for a moment?"

Baby T gathered the dirt in an obscure corner and placed the broom beside it neatly. Then made to leave the room for Madam and Mr. F.

"Oh, don't go. Stay. It's you he wants to consult with."

It was the first time Maami Broni gave Baby T a hand-me down. And by the time Mr. F was finished with Baby T, Maami Broni knew that she had been lied to. Baby T cried so much that Maami Broni let her go the next twenty-four hours without another backpass. She was a seasoned Madam, but she was first a woman with feminine urges. Yet, though she may have desired to let Baby T off, the decision was no longer hers. Poison was the boss. Only he could let Baby T go.

Maami Broni helped in the only way she knew how. She introduced her to the 'devil's weed'. It helped. Once Baby T began to use it regularly, carrying out her 'duty' with several men night and day became bearable. The men liked her. She was pretty and young. Everything was going 'fine' . . . till Onko went and consulted a jujuman to help pull his business out of its slumber. And once the first headache with the pure white home bred fowl had been conveniently solved by the jujuman, the next one reared its ugly head.

How the hell was he going to get a piece of Baby T's pubic hair?

25

The Agboo Ayee drinking spot kiosk, by a freak coincidence, was of the same blue colour as the Rasta hairdresser's kiosk at Agbogbloshie. For the past almost three weeks, its first customer of the day had been Kpakpo. He was also always the last man to leave. There was even talk that sometimes, for lack of a place to go, Kpakpo slept right beside the gutter behind the kiosk. Since he walked out of Maa Tsuru's life, the more he was determined to stay out of it, and the more he realized how he had grown attached to her. Yet how could he return and stick around her when Fofo had complicated things by bringing in those organization people and that radio station man?

He heard his name mentioned. It sounded afar. The kiosk owner said, "That's him over there!"

Kpakpo heard footsteps approach him. He looked up into the figure's face. It looked familiar. He checked the feet. The man's steps. He knew those feet. He looked up again. It struck home. "You?"

"Yes, me. I have been looking all over for you."

"For what? To help you redeem your lost business? Is it true what I heard? That it has gone down, down, down?"

"That is why I have been on the lookout for you. Take two tots on my account." He called the spot owner. "Give Kpakpo two tots. I'll pay. When he is done, give him another two tots."

By the time Kpakpo had quaffed ten tots, all Onko needed to

do was to have issued any order, and Kpakpo would have even done the 'breakdance' for him.

All this while, Onko had taken in not one drop of anything.

"Kpakpo!" Onko launched his plan; "I want you to take me to Poison."

Kpakpo was drunk all right. Ten tots of *akpeteshie* quaffed in less than an hour, even under Siberian conditions, was bound to hit home fast, let alone inside a stuffy two by four wooden kiosk in hot humid Accra. Yet, with the mention of Poison, Kpakpo's mind reeled to attention.

"Me? Take you to Poison? Onko, do you think that I am so boozed that you can sing me 'Lead kindly light' and set me on the path to my grave without me knowing? Do I look to you to be like someone in the mood for death? Are you looking for a sacrificial goat?"

"Then help me get to him!" Onko urged him. And shouted to the kiosk owner, "Give Kpakpo another two tots on my account, please." Then he dipped his hand into his trouser pocket; brought out some notes; and pushed them into Kpakpo's shirt pocket.

Kpakpo stared at the glass he had just emptied, then at the notes inside his pocket, then Onko's face. "What is this you are asking me to do?" he whined at Onko.

Onko said without pretence, "I am desperate."

Kpakpo's head hung in anguish. "I can't take you to him, but I can show you the way to Mama Abidjan. Give her some money and she will take you to him. She knows about you so she might be reluctant initially to co-operate with you. So show her the money first before you tell her what you want from her. It's all about money. Have you got it? Money?"

"I came prepared." Onko replied. "I have put together everything that I have. I even sold some personal things to raise additional money."

Mama Abidjan scowled at the sight of Onko. After all, just because a child is doing his own thing on a chamber pot does not mean he is immune to the stench of the contents in another's chamberpot placed under his nose. Or?

"What do you want here?" she snapped at Onko.

Onko kept faith with Kpakpo's advice. He stretched out the wad of notes. Mama Abidjan's eyes moved to and remained transfixed on it. Then she glanced sharply at Onko in the face and returned the gaze to the cash. "What is this for?" she sniped eventually.

Onko didn't reply immediately. He took Mama Abidjan's hand and carefully placed the cash in her palm. "Recommend me to Poison as a possible good client." He told her. "I will pay good. I will be a regular client. I want her. I love her. I want my Baby T."

Baby T's reaction at the sight of Onko, churned Maami Broni's heart. She concealed it because Poison was present.

"I anticipated something like this, after all that I learnt from Mama Abidjan." Poison disclosed to Onko. "That was why I accompanied you here personally. It was worth my time, considering you intend to become one of my regulars. But it will cost you extra."

"I'll pay!" Onko replied.

After having been with so many clients over the course of time, no wonder it took only seasoned Poison to anticipate such a possible reaction from Baby T. Maami Broni for all the experience she had gathered in her 'working life' did not envisage that the man Baby T and her sister had trusted so much, who was to them like the Uncle they never had, but who turned round to do something so wrong and so terrible, could still affect Baby T so much. Her crying and hysteria however, began to get on Poison's nerves. He made Onko an offer. "Maami Broni is not my only partner. I have other partners with equally young and pretty 'pupils' like Baby T. If she doesn't want you, I can take you around to have a look at the others."

Onko shook his head vehemently. "It's her or no one. I have already offered to double the charge, haven't I? I am tripling it!"

And under Poison's eagle greedy eyes, counted more money.

Poison saw red. He snatched the extra money from Onko and entered the room.

"You either agree to give him pleasure or I'll remove you from here and put you to work at 'Circle!'" he threatened Baby T.

Work at Circle was pure hell inside out. The girls there had to be more rough and aggressive to fish out clients and potential clients themselves, unlike as pertained at Maami Broni's, where the clients came to Baby T. Occasionally, there were police swoops, which in themselves were very disconcerting. A girl could sometimes make the mistake of misjudging a very regular man for a potential client and receive for her misdirected efforts, insults and threats or occasionally even some slaps. Then there were the catfights between the girls themselves over clients. It was risky and dangerous at 'Circle'. A few times a girl had gone off with a client only for her body to be later found dumped somewhere. A client a girl went away with could also be a 'brokeman' on the lookout for some fast money. After satisfying himself therefore with her, not only would he refuse to pay for her services, but would rob her of her earnings too. Yet, if on top of all this, a girl was owned by a streetlord, she had to make a certain amount of money for him also; rain or shine. In the milieu therefore, to work or be put to work at Circle, and go after men instead of men coming to you like as was with Baby T at Maami Broni's place, meant you were chaff. A 'has-been'.

Baby T had youth and beauty on her side. And a 'good' reputation too. She was no chaff. "I won't go to Circle!" she cried at Poison.

"Then serve him!" Poison ordered.

"No!"

"Why?"

"I won't!"

Wham! The first slap landed. Another followed in quick sucession. Baby T felt the right side of her face go momentarily numb.

"I said serve him!"

"I won't!"

Poison's face went bland. Maami Broni always cringed at the sight of that. Strange old thoughts went through Poison's mind to manifest themselves in that facial transformation. Thoughts of little him quivering before his grinning stepfather who was about to enjoy his hobby of inflicting pain on the little helpless boy. But Poison had long ceased to be that little boy who suffered at the hands of his stepfather in the presence of his frightened and help-less mother. Ever since graduating to the fearless streetlord that he had become, Poison, in his psyche, had become the stepfather. He no longer suffered the pain. He inflicted it.

As he stared blandly at Baby T, he slowly unbuckled his leather belt and drew it rhythmically out through the trousers hooks ...

Baby T felt only the first lash, which landed across her shoul-ders. The right side of her face felt dead already anyway. She sim-ply imagined the rest of her body also dead.

"Don't you ever dare challenge me again!" Poison warned when he was through with her.

Baby T heard it faintly. It was as if through a maze. She felt a strange reverberation in her left ear and a bizarre stillness in the right.

She was huddled in the corner when Maami Broni and Onko en-tered the room. Her thin blouse was stuck to her body with her tears. Maami Broni turned and walked out of the room. She couldn't utter a word. She left Onko in there with Baby T and locked the door from outside; and took a seat beside the door. When Onko was finished with Baby T, he would tap for the door to be opened.

226

The tap sounded a little too early and a bit too frantic. Onko had given up, she thought. She opened the door. Onko did not step out as Maami Broni had expected. He beckoned her in.

Baby T was lying with a split head on the concrete floor. A bizarre image came to Maami Broni's mind. It was the image of splintered stone oozing blood. A stone struck against steel.

Baby T was dead.

....

EPILOGUE

The weight of Baby T's spirit on her mind, Onko's suicide, and Sylv Po's persistent pleas on air; all combined, pushed Maami Broni out from her hideout to Harvest FM.

Fofo by then had reported to the organization to begin her rehabilitation. Her test results from Korle-Bu were still not in, but she knew that MUTE would be there for her. That was consoling. She could also mourn her sister openly. That felt good.

Sylv Po drew up his questionnaire for the bodies and organizations and the Justice Ministry, on the 'oldest child's' case. His hopes diminished more by each new day. Preliminary enquiries made by him indicated that, within the existing legal parameters, there was nothing that could be done to stop parents from bringing forth more children even though they clearly could not cater for them. One woman interviewed by Sylv Po on the issue at the Agbogbloshie market, first pronounced proudly that she had already made nine children ranging from between one and fourteen years and was anxiously aiming for baby number ten.

Asked how the nine children were faring, she shrugged and replied, "They are there. God is taking care of them." Then to the 'oldest child's' issue, she snapped, "Nonsense! Children of today don't respect. Does she want the court to order her father to stop sleeping with his wife?"

Maami Broni made further revelations.

It was Poison who ordered that the gang dump Baby T's body behind the Rasta kiosk at Agbogbloshie in the night. The facial mutilations were to confuse identification. That way, she could pass for a *kayayoo* from the north. The shaven hairs were to lend weight to the theory of her death being her punishment for adultery. That was why the *kayayoos* were warned not to talk. They could have divulged that the dead girl was not one of them and therefore not a girl called Fati.

"Was it you who called to rebuff the Fati story?" Sylv Po asked.

"Yes." Maami Broni responded.

"Why?"

"Why? You are asking me why? My brother, I have been in this business since Sodom and Gomorrah catapulted from the pages of the Old Testament to superimpose itself at *Agbobloshie*. I have seen and done everything that any seasoned woman in this trade could see and do. Everything! But never has a life been ended in my room. Never! The image has never left me. Not once since it happened have I known peace or sleep. When I am bathing, I am afraid to close my eyes. I see her everywhere. I hear sounds. I feel her unseen presence. Poison couldn't care less when I told him. He warned me to pull myself together and stop acting like a child. He wasn't the one hearing the sounds in the head and feeling the weight of Baby T's spirit. I was on my own in this. I could have prayed to God for help but how would I have dared? How could I dare pray for help and forgiveness for a deed like this? I sacrificed the fowls, one in my room and the other at where her body was dumped. I mixed the two bloods. Her blood and that of the sacrifices. It should have stopped the sounds and lifted her unseen weight, but it did not work. I continued to see images of the splintered stone oozing blood. Her spirit is seated inside my head like a chief in state. She is with me wherever I go. Maybe now that I have come forth and talked, it will go away. The weight of her spirit will be lifted. Do you think it will go away?"

Sylv Po replied calmly, "You know something? Have that dialogue you've been afraid to have with the Old Man upstairs."

Maami Broni scowled. "Who?"

"God. That prayer of forgiveness. Maybe then, if He senses true regret in your heart, He will make the sound of stone against steel inside your head go away. Then the weight of her spirit will also be lifted.

Kabria woke up in middle of the night sweating profusely. She had been toying with the idea of whether the time had not really come for her to finally, truly finally get rid of Creamy and maybe coax Adade to top up whatever she would get for Creamy to enable her buy a second hand 'Daewoo Tico'. Creamy sensed its Madam's thoughts. It felt sad and tackled things its own way. It implanted itself into Kabria's dream. And what an implantation it was.

In Kabria's dream, someone offered to buy Creamy off her hands and made her a very generous offer. An overjoyed Kabria patted Creamy's dashboard fondly for the last time and bid it adieus. Creamy's new owner drove it away. He had plans for the old Beetle.

The following day, something bizarre happened. Creamy materialized back in the house, parked at its exact spot. The buyer called Kabria. He was shaken and hysterical. Creamy just took off by itself, he claimed. He ran after it and tried to catch up with it, but the nearer he got to Creamy, the faster it drove itself away. Could Kabria be honest with him and confess to him the juju insurance she took on Creamy?

"Adade!" Kabria screamed at this juncture, "I just had a terrible dream about Creamy."

"Good for you!" Adade snapped.

He never really got over that night he arrived home and found that Kabria had gone out. A night that Ottu rather audaciously had told him to the face that, well, they had all agreed in the car on their way home from school that, if they needed something which any of the children would normally have asked to be carried out by Kabria, well, they would ask Daddy to do, because he was to be both 'Mummy' and 'Daddy' in one for that night, as Mummy had so often had had to be in Daddy's absence. For this reason, Adade, who was used to having his briefcase taken from him at the door on arriving home, while he strode in leisurely to slump on the sofa and moan about how tired he was, to Kabria's ever ready to listen ears, found himself having to take care not only of himself but the children too. Why therefore should he, just when he was back to settling comfortably into 'normalcy', listen to a dream about Creamy?

It was after midnight when Kabria finally went back to sleep, by which time, Sodom and Gomorrah had just awakened and gearing up to life.

....

Breinigsville, PA USA
26 January 2011
254190BV00003B/6/A